Hiram Corson

Primer of English Verse

Chiefly in its æsthetic and organic character

Hiram Corson

Primer of English Verse
Chiefly in its æsthetic and organic character

ISBN/EAN: 9783337424503

Printed in Europe, USA, Canada, Australia, Japan

Cover: Foto ©Andreas Hilbeck / pixelio.de

More available books at **www.hansebooks.com**

A

PRIMER OF ENGLISH VERSE

CHIEFLY IN ITS ÆSTHETIC AND
ORGANIC CHARACTER

BY

HIRAM CORSON, LL.D.

PROFESSOR OF ENGLISH LITERATURE IN THE CORNELL UNIVERSITY

BOSTON, U.S.A.

PUBLISHED BY GINN & COMPANY

1893

TABLE OF CONTENTS.

———•••———

A PRIMER OF ENGLISH VERSE.

I.

POETIC UNITIES AND THEIR ORIGIN.

THE principal coefficients of poetic expression are Rhythm, Metre, Stanza, Rhyme, Assonance, Alliteration, Melody, and Harmony, which seem to be all due, when they are vital and organic, to *the unifying action of feeling or emotion*. When strong feeling is in any way objectified, a unifying process sets in. The insulated intellect, in *its* action, tends rather in an opposite direction — that is, in an analytic direction. It matters not upon *what* feeling or emotion is projected, or with what it is incorporated; it will be found that in all cases it is unifying or, to use a word coined by Coleridge, *esemplastic*, in its action. If we look at a landscape coldly or indifferently, we may be cognizant of its various elements or phases; but there is little or no effort to grasp it as a *whole*, and to subject all its elements to some principle of harmony or fusion. At another time, when our feelings are active, and the intellect is in a more or less negative state, there will be a spontaneous and, it may be, a quite unconscious effort to *unify* that same landscape,

1

to subject all its elements to some principle of harmony — to fuse the primal units, so to speak, into one complex unit. It may be that the landscape is composed of very incongruous elements; but even then, the feelings, if abnormally active, by reason of some associations either of pleasure or pain, or from some other cause, may project upon it a light or a shade that will bind together its otherwise inharmonious features.

Now as soon as feeling is embodied in speech, and to the degree to which it is embodied, we find that speech is worked up, more or less distinctly or emphatically, into unities of various kinds. The primal unit, the unit of measure, we call *foot*, which is made up of two or more vocal impulses, according to the nature of the feeling which evolves it. This primal unit is combined into a higher unity, which is called *verse*, and this, in its turn, is combined into a still higher unity, which is called *stanza*, and so on. Rhythm is a succession and involution of unities, that is, unities within unities. The term is as applicable to a succession of verses as to a succession of feet, and to a succession of stanzas as to a succession of verses.

II.

ENFORCING, FUSING, AND COMBINING PRINCIPLES
OF POETIC UNITIES.

a. ACCENT.

NOW we find that each class of unities has its
enforcing, or fusing, or combining principle —
the agency by which it is more or less strongly marked
and individualized; that of the primal unit, foot, we
call *accent*. What accent really is, it does not now
concern us to consider. There is not a general agree-
ment among prosodists as to *what* it really is. But
whatever it is, whether the vowel or syllable on which
it occurs is distinguished from the rest of the word
by an increased sharpness of tone, or by an increased
force or loudness, or whether it unites both, it is a
sufficiently valid phenomenon, for any one with ears
to appreciate its function in modern verse. When
the following lines are pronounced, everybody knows
which syllables are distinguished by the accent:

At the close of the day, when the hamlet is still,
And mortals the sweets of forgetfulness prove,
When naught but the torrent is heard on the hill,
And naught but the nightingale's song in the grove, etc.

Every kind of foot consists of one, and only one,
accented syllable and one or two unaccented. The
principal feet in English verse are:

3

1. An accented syllable preceded by one unaccented;

2. An accented syllable followed by one unaccented;

3. An accented syllable preceded by two unaccented;

4. An accented syllable followed by two unaccented;

5. An accented syllable preceded and followed by an unaccented.

If a be used to represent an accented syllable, and x, an unaccented, these several feet may be indicated as follows: 1, xa; 2, ax; 3, xxa; 4, axx; 5, xax.[1]

A verse consisting of two feet, or measures, is called a dimeter; of three, a trimeter; of four, a tetrameter; of five, a pentameter; of six, a hexameter; and so on. An xa pentameter may be indicated as a 5xa; an ax tetrameter, as a 4ax; an xxa tetrameter, as a 4xxa; an axx dimeter, as a 2axx; and so on.

A stanza consisting of four 5xa verses, that of Gray's 'Elegy,' for example, may be indicated as 4 (5xa). A sonnet may be indicated as 14(5xa); the Spenserian stanza, as 8(5xa)   6xa.

b. MELODY.

The fusing or combining principle or agency of a verse is *Melody*. We often meet with verses which scan, as we say, all right, and yet we feel that they have no vitality as verses. This may, in most cases, be

---

[1] This is Latham's method of metrical notation, in his 'Handbook of the English Language.'

attributed to their purely mechanical or cold-blooded
structure.   They are not the product of feeling, which
attracts to itself (a great fact) vocal elements, either
vowels or consonants, which chime well together, and
in accord with the feeling; but they are rather the
product of literary skill.   The writer had no song, no
music in his soul, when he composed them, and he
should have written, if he wrote at all, in straight-
forward prose.   But when we read such verses as the
following, we know what must have been back of
their composition :

> How sweet the moonlight sleeps upon this bank !
> Here will we sit, and let the sounds of music
> Creep in our ears : soft stillness and the night
> Become the touches of sweet harmony.
> > —*Merchant of Venice,* 5. 1. 54-57.

> Not wholly in the busy world, nor quite
> Beyond it, blooms the garden that I love.
> News from the humming city comes to it
> In sound of funeral or of marriage bells :
> And, sitting muffled in dark leaves, you hear
> The windy clanging of the minster clock ;
> Although between it and the garden lies
> A league of grass, washed by a slow broad stream,
> That, stirred with languid pulses of the oar,
> Waves all its lazy lilies, and creeps on,
> Barge-laden, to three arches of a bridge
> Crowned with the minster towers.   The fields between
> Are dewy fresh, browsed by deep-uddered kine,
> And all about, the large lime feathers low,
> The lime, a summer home of murmurous wings.
> > — TENNYSON'S *The Gardener's Daughter; or, the Pictures.*

> Oh, good gigantic smile o' the brown old earth,
> This autumn morning !   How he sets his bones

To bask i' the sun, and thrusts out knees and feet
For the ripple to run over in its mirth;
Listening the while, where on the heap of stones
The white breast of the sea-lark twitters sweet.
— Browning's *James Lee's Wife*. VII. *Among the Rocks.*

With heart as calm as lakes that sleep,
    In frosty moonlight glistening;
Or mountain rivers, where they creep
Along a channel smooth and deep,
    To their own far-off murmurs listening.
Wordsworth's *Memory* (7th Stanza).

And Arthur came, and labouring up the pass,
All in a misty moonshine, unawares
Had trodden that crowned skeleton, and the skull
Brake from the nape, and from the skull the crown
Rolled into light, and turning on its rims,
Fled like a glittering rivulet to the tarn:
And down the shingly scaur he plunged, and caught,
And set it on his head, and in his heart
Heard murmurs, Lo, thou likewise shalt be king.
— Tennyson's *Elaine*

The lights begin to twinkle from the rocks:
The long day wanes: the slow moon climbs; the deep
Moans round with many voices.
Tennyson's *Ulysses*

The mountain wooded to the peak, the lawns
And winding glades high up like ways to Heaven,
The slender coco's drooping crown of plumes,
The lightning flash of insect and of bird,
The lustre of the long convolvuluses
That coiled around the stately stems, and ran
Ev'n to the limit of the land, the glows
And glories of the broad belt of the world,
All these he saw; but what he fain had seen
He could not see, the kindly human face,
Nor ever hear a kindly voice, but heard

The myriad shriek of wheeling ocean-fowl,
The league-long roller thundering on the reef,
The moving whisper of huge trees that branched
And blossomed in the zenith, or the sweep
Of some precipitous rivulet to the wave,
As down the shore he ranged, or all day long
Sat often in the seaward-gazing gorge,
A shipwrecked sailor, waiting for a sail:
No sail from day to day, but every day
The sunrise broken into scarlet shafts
Among the palms and ferns and precipices;
The blaze upon the waters to the east;
The blaze upon his island overhead;
The blaze upon the waters to the west;
Then the great stars that globed themselves in Heaven,
The hollower-bellowing ocean, and again
The scarlet shafts of sunrise — but no sail.
— TENNYSON'S *Enoch Arden.*

Now came still evening on, and twilight gray
Had in her sober livery all things clad:
Silence accompanied: for beast and bird,
They to their grassy couch, these to their nests,
Were slunk, all but the wakeful nightingale:
She all night long her amorous descant sung:
Silence was pleased.   Now glowed the firmament
With living sapphires: Hesperus, that led
The starry host, rode brightest, till the Moon,
Rising in clouded majesty, at length
Apparent queen, unveiled her peerless light,
And o'er the dark her silver mantle threw.
— *Paradise Lost,* iv. 598-609.

Immediately the mountains huge appear
Emergent, and their broad bare backs upheave
Into the clouds; their tops ascend the sky:
So high as heaved the tumid hills, so low
Down sunk a hollow bottom broad and deep,
Capacious bed of waters: thither they

Hasted with glad precipitance, uprolled
As drops on dust conglobing from the dry;
Part rise in crystal wall, or ridge direct,
For haste; such flight the great command impressed
On the swift floods: as armies at the call
Of trumpet (for of armies thou hast heard)
Troop to their standard, so the watery throng,
Wave rolling after wave, where way they found,
If steep, with torrent rapture, if thro' plain,
Soft-ebbing: nor withstood them rock or hill,
But they, or under ground, or circuit wide
With serpent error wandering, found their way,
And on the washy ooze deep channels wore.[1]

> — *Paradise Lost*, vii. 285-303.

Light thickens, and the crow
Makes wing to the rooky wood:
Good things of day begin to droop and drowse,
Whiles night's black agents to their preys do rouse.

> — SHAKESPEARE'S *Macbeth*, 3. 2. 50-53.

Not poppy, nor mandragora,
Nor all the drowsy syrups of the world,
Shall ever medicine thee to that sweet sleep
Which thou owedst yesterday.

> SHAKESPEARE'S *Othello*, 3. 3. 330-313.

The busy larke, messager of daye,
Salueth in hire song the morwe gray;
And fyry Phebus ryseth up so bright,
That al the orient laugheth of the light,
And with his stremes dryeth in the greves
The silver dropes, hongyng on the leeves.

> — CHAUCER'S C. T., 1491 F 1498 (Harleian text).

Such passages as these the student should memorize, and frequently repeat, if he would cultivate a
sense of melody and harmony

[1] See Genesis i. 9

The principles of melodious combinations of vowels have not yet been established, so far as it is within the possibilities of analysis to establish them. But any one with an ear for vowel melody can appreciate it in a verse, and could distinguish, perhaps, nice degrees of melody in a number of given verses ranging through a pretty wide gamut. But he would not be able to set forth all the secrets of the different degrees of melody. Yet these secrets are, to some extent, within the possibilities of analysis. A noting of all the more musical lines of Shakespeare, and of a few other great authors, might lead to valuable results toward determining more of the secrets of melodious fusion than we yet possess.

The melody secured through consonants is, to the general ear, more readily appreciable, and can be more easily explained. Much of it has a physiological basis, depending on the greater or less ease with which the organs of speech articulate certain successive consonants. Though the vowel element plays the main part in the melody and harmony of verse (representing, as it does, the more spiritual element of form), all the great English poets from Chaucer to Tennyson make frequent and effective use of alliteration. It veins the entire surface of English poetry to an extent but little suspected by most readers.

There is a great deal of effective alliteration which passes unnoticed by reason of its being upon internal, instead of initial, consonants. It contributes, nevertheless, to the melodious fusion of the verse, though it may entirely evade the consciousness as an element of the melody.

From a remark which Chaucer puts into the mouth of his Parson, it has been wrongly inferred that he (Chaucer) had a contempt for alliteration. The Parson says, in the Prologue to his Tale, 'I can not geste — rom, ram, ruf — by lettre'; but in the next line, he adds, ' Ne, god wot, rym holde I but litel bettre.'

So it might be as fairly inferred that Chaucer held rhyme in small esteem. But all the 'Canterbury Tales' are in rhyme, except the Parson's Tale, and the Tale of Meliboeus, which the poet himself is supposed to tell. However Chaucer may have regarded alliteration (it may have been in his mind, it certainly was, identified with the literature which was nearest the people), his own poetry is delicately veined with it throughout. I have noted all the passages in the Canterbury Tales' where it distinctly contributes to the melody and the resultant suggestiveness of his verse, and such passages number 326. In the description of the tournament n the Knight's Tale of ' Palamon and Arcite,' he uses it with a vigor of effect not surpassed in English poetry:

> The heraldz laften here prikyng up and doun ;
> Now ryngede the tromp and clarioun .
> Ther is nomore to say, but est and west
> In gon the speres ful sadly in arest ;
> In goth the scharpe spore into the side.
> Ther seen men who can juste and who can ryde ;
> Ther schyveren schaftes upon scheeldes thykke ;
> He feeleth thurgh the herte-spon the prikke.
> Up springen spere twenty foot on highte .
> Out goon the swerdes as the silver brighte

The helmes thei to-hewen and to-schrede ;
Out brest the blood, with sterne stremes reede.
With mighty maces the bones thay to-breste.
He thurgh the thikkeste of the throng gan threste.
Ther stomblen steedes stronge, and doun goon alle.
He rolleth under foot as doth a balle.
He foyneth on his feet with his tronchoun,
And he him hurtleth with his hors adoun.

— *C. T.*, 2601-18.

The alliteration in this passage is *organic;* that is, it is an inseparable part of the expression.

The general character of Chaucer's alliterations is shown in the following verses or bits of verses. Though simple and unobtrusive, they make, here and there, a flitting contribution to the melody of his verse, without, in the least, obtruding themselves upon the consciousness of the reader : smale foweles maken melodye 1 :9;[1] to seken straunge strondes 1 : 13 ; And though that he were worthy he was wys And of his port as meeke as is a mayde 3 :68, 69; Al ful of fresshe flowres whyte and reede 3 :90; And frenssh she spak ful faire and fetisly 4 : 124; A manly man to been an Abbot able 5 : 167; whan he rood men myghte his brydel heere Gynglen in a whistlynge wynd als cleere And eek as loude as dooth the Chapel belle 5 : 169-171 ; She hadde passed many a straunge strem 14 : 464; fful longe were his legges and ful lene 17 : 591 ; ffulfild of Ire and of Iniquitee 28 : 940; ther daweth hym no day 48 : 1676; With hunte and horn and houndes hym bisyde 49 : 1678 ; Thebes with hise olde walles wyde 54 : 1880; With knotty knarry

---

[1] The first number indicates the page of the Six-Text Print of the 'Canterbury Tales,' and the second number the verse.

bareyne trees olde 57:1977; The open werre with
woundes al bibledde 58:202; Armed ful wel with
hertes stierne and stoute 62:2154; Hir body wessh
with water of a welle 65:2283; And for to walken
in the wodes wilde 66:2309; oon of the fyres queynte
And quyked agayn 67:2334, 5; Of faire yonge
fresshe Venus free 68:2386; As fayn as fowel is of
the brighte sonne 70:2437; to the paleys rood ther
many a route Of lordes 71:2494; His hardy herte
myghte hym helpe naught 76:2649; His brest to-
brosten with his sadel bowe 77:2691; That dwelled
in his herte syk and soore 80:2804; That in that
selue groue swoote and grene 82:2860; The grete
toures se we wane and wende 86:3025; His rode
was reed hise eyen greye as goos 95:3317; sat ay as
stille as stoon 100:3472; by hym that harwed helle
101:3512; so wilde and wood 3517; I am thy trewe
verray wedded wyf 103:3609; He wepeth weyleth
maketh sory cheere He siketh with ful many a sory
swogh 104:3618, 19; Wery and weet as beest is in
the reyn 118:4107; And forth she sailleth in the
salte see 144:445; Er that the wilde wawes wol hire
dryue 144:468; tellen plat and pleyn 158:886; She
lighte doun and falleth hym to feete 165:1104; His
fader was a man ful free 191:1911; fful many a
mayde bright in bour 192:1932; He priketh thurgh
a fair forest, 1944; By dale and eek by downe 193:
1986; And priketh ouer stile and stoon 194:1988;
Toward his weddyng walkynge by the weye 257:
3216; ffortune was first freend and sitthe foo 279:
3013. In pacience ladde a ful symple lyf 283:4016;
Whoch causeth folk to dreden in hir dremes 286:4119;

His herte bathed in a bath of blisse 370 : 1253 ; the foule feend me fecche 380 : 1610 ; With scrippe and tipped staf ytukked hye In euery hous he gan to poure and prye 386 : 1737, 38 ; as light as leef on lynde 441 : 1211 ; To lede in ese and hoolynesse his lyf 453 : 1628 ; He wepeth and he wayleth pitously 466 : 2072 ; Seken in euery halke and euery herne 511 : 1121 ; That swich a Monstre or merueille myghte be 517 : 1344.

These examples will suffice to show the character of Chaucer's alliterations. The greater part of them may have been written unconsciously by the poet ; his sense of melody often attracting words with the same initial or internal consonants, as well as asso-nantal words, — all contributing, more or less, to the general melody and harmony. Feeling, according to its character, weaves its own vowel and consonantal texture.

It was Spenser who first, to any extent, exhibited organic alliteration. Alliteration, as employed in Anglo-Saxon poetry,[1] and in the 'Vision of William concerning Piers the Plowman,' being, as it is, constantly kept up, is generally a mere mechanical device ; and where it *is* organically employed, it loses, in consequence of its constant use, its effect as an exceptional consonantal melody.

---

[1] Professor Earle, in his 'Philology of the English Tongue,' says, in somewhat high style, 'The alliteration of the Saxon poetry not only gratified the ear with a resonance like that of modern rhyme, but it also had the rhetorical advantage of touching the emphatic words ; falling as it did on the natural summits of the construction, and tingeing them with the brilliance of a musical reverberation.'

There is not much of it in the poor poetry of the interval of nearly two hundred years between the death of Chaucer and the appearance of the 'Faerie Queene'; and, probably, if the 'Faerie Queene' had not been written, alliteration would have been a much less notable feature of English Poetry. Only a poet with the rare metrical sensibility of Spenser could have taught subsequent poets its subtler capabilities. Readers of modern poetry are, perhaps, not generally aware of what a great, though secret, power, alliteration is, in all the best poets from Spenser to Tennyson. I do not mean to say that its effect is not felt; for if it were not, what would be the good of it? but the *source* of the effect is not generally observed.

Shakespeare employs alliteration, as he does every other element of expressiveness, that is, just where he should employ it, and nowhere else. It sometimes gives the *toning* to an entire passage; while at the same time it does not obtrude itself upon the consciousness; as, for example, in the speech of Oberon to Puck, in 'A Midsummer-Night's Dream,' 2. 1. 148–164:

My gentle Puck, come hither   Thou rememberest
Since once I sat upon a promontory,
And heard a mermaid on a dolphin's back
Uttering such dulcet and harmonious breath
That the rude sea grew civil at her song
And certain stars shot madly from their spheres,
To hear the sea maid's music.
        Puck.   I remember.
        Obe.   That very time I saw, but thou couldst not,
Flying between the cold moon and the earth,

Cupid all armed : a certain aim he took
At a fair vestal throned by the west,
And loosed his love-shaft smartly from his bow,
As it should pierce a hundred thousand hearts :
But I might see young Cupid's fiery shaft
Quenched in the chaste beams of the watery moon,
And the imperial votaress passed on
In maiden meditation, fancy-free.[1]

But to determine its full importance as an element
of melody, there should be a careful noting of all its
more incidental effects throughout his plays, such as
these, for example :

As if an angel *d*ropped *d*own from the clouds,
To turn and *w*ind a fiery Pegasus,
And *w*itch the *w*orld with noble horsemanship.
— *1 Henry IV*. 4. 1. 108–110.

*H*arry to *H*arry shall, *h*ot *h*orse to *h*orse,
Meet, and ne'er part, till one *d*rop *d*own a corse.
— 4. 1. 122, 123.

And *d*eeper than *d*id ever plummet sound
I'll *d*rown my book.
— *Tempest* 5. 1. 56, 57.

That *t*ips with silver all these frui*t*-*t*ree-*t*ops.
— *Romeo and Juliet*, 2. 2. 108.

S*t*ands *t*ip-*t*oe on the *m*isty *m*oun*t*ain *t*ops.
— 3. 5. 10.

*H*unting thee *h*ence with *h*unts-up to the day.
— 3. 5. 34.

[1] The mechanical use of alliteration as distinguished from its organic
use is humorously and satirically exhibited in various passages in his plays.
See L. L. L. 4. 2. 58–64; M. N. D. 1. 2. 33–40; L. L. L. 3. 1. 181–185;
Tam. of S. 3. 2. 53 *et seq.*, ' sped with spavins ' etc. R. & J., 2. 4. 41
et seq., ' Laura to his lady ' etc. Oth. 1. 1. 112 *et seq.*, ' you'll have
your nephews neigh to you ' etc. Oth. 2. 3. 79. (cited in 'The
Shakespeare Key,' by Charles and Mary Cowden Clarke, pp. 23, 24).

The translators of the King James's Bible sometimes make an effective use of it: *e.g.*, Ps. civ. 3, 4: 'Who layeth the beams of his chambers in the waters: who maketh the clouds his chariot: who walketh upon the wings of the wind: who maketh his angels spirits: his ministers a flaming fire.'

There is an interwoven alliteration of *f*, *b*, and *d*, in the following, from the Song of Deborah and Barak, Judges v. 27:

'At her *f*eet he *b*owed, he *f*ell, he lay *d*own: at her feet he *b*owed, he *f*ell: where he *b*owed, there he *f*ell *d*own *d*ead.'

Tennyson employs alliteration with that rare artistic skill so characteristic of him. It is generally so worked up with other elements of his melody that it is not noticed or felt as a distinct element. But he sometimes, for some special enforcement, brings it prominently forward in his verse. This is especially so in 'The Princess' and in 'Maud.'

Some of the Songs in 'The Princess,' which come in after the several sections of the poem, owe their toning largely to alliteration and assonance, and to the repetition of the same words. 'The Cradle Song,' 'Sweet and low, sweet and low,' after the second section, and the 'Bugle Song,' 'The splendor falls on castle walls,' after the third section, are examples.

Some of the poet's most effective alliterations occur in 'Maud':

The red ribbed ledges drip with a silent horror of blood.

And ever he *m*uttered and *m*addened, and ever *w*anned *w*ith despair,
And out he *w*alked when the *w*ind like a broken *w*orldling *w*ailed
And the flying gold of the ruined *w*ood-lands drove thro' the air.

And my pulses closed their gates with a *sh*ock on my heart as I heard
The *sh*rill-edged *sh*riek of a mother divide the *sh*uddering night.

And lust of gain in the spirit of Cain, is it better or worse
Than the *h*eart of the citizen *hi*ssing in war on *h*is own *h*earth-stone?

*M*ay *m*ake my heart as a *m*illstone, set my *f*ace as a *f*lint,
*Ch*eat and be *ch*eated, and die: who knows? we are ashes and dust.

When the poor are *h*ovelled and *h*ustled together, each *s*ex, like *s*wine,
When only the *l*edger *l*ives, and when only not all men *l*ie.

To *p*estle a *p*oisoned *p*oison behind his crimson lights.

And *r*ave at the *l*ie and the *l*iar, ah God, as he used to *r*ave.

*W*ere it not *w*ise if I *f*led *f*rom the *p*lace and the *p*it and the *f*ear?

Cold and *c*lear-*c*ut face, why come you so *c*ruelly meek?

*W*alked in a *w*intry *w*ind by a ghastly glimmer and found
The shining *d*affo*d*il *d*ead, and Orion low in his grave.

The *s*ilent *s*apphire-*s*pangled marriage ring of the land?

But *s*orrow *s*eize me if ever that *l*ight be my *l*eading star!

Your *m*other is *m*ute in her grave as her i*m*age in *m*arble above:
Your father is ever in London, you *w*ander about at your *w*ill:
You have but fed on the roses, and *l*ain in the *l*ilies of *l*ife.

The following from the 'Morte d'Arthur' are effective:

> and over them the *sea*-wind *s*ang
> Shrill, chill, with *f*lakes of *f*oam.

> I heard the *r*ipple washing in the *r*eeds,
> And the *w*ild *w*ater lapping on the crag.

> So *f*lashed and *f*ell the brand Excalibur.

> The *b*are *b*lack *cl*iff *cl*anged round him.

But the use of vowels as a means of producing that musical accompaniment to thought, through which a poet voices his feelings and sympathies, and makes spiritual suggestions, demands a far subtler sense of spiritual affinities.   This subtler sense was possessed, in an eminent degree, by Samuel Taylor Coleridge; and he has most strikingly revealed it in the First Part of his 'Christabel,' and in his 'Kubla Khan.' In the former poem, he has signally illustrated the truth of a marginal note which he wrote in a copy of Selden's 'Table Talk,' on this sentence: 'Verses prove nothing but the quantity of syllables; they are not meant for logic.' 'True,' writes Coleridge, 'they, that is, verses, are not logic, but they are, or ought to be, the *envoys* and *representatives* of that vital passion which is the practical cement of logic, and, without which, logic must remain inert.'   A profound remark.

The following are notable examples:

> The lady sprang up suddenly,
> The lovely lady, Christabel!
> It moaned as near, as near can be,
> But what it is she cannot tell
> On the other side it seems to be,
> Of the huge, broad-breasted, old oak tree.

The form of this stanza is quite perfect. Note the
suggestiveness of the abrupt vowels in the first verse,
the abatement required for the proper elocution, in
the second verse, the prolongable vowels and sub-
vowels of the third, and then the short vowels again
in the fourth. Then note how the vowels in the last
verse swell responsive to the poet's conception ; and
how encased they are in a strong framework of consonants.

> The night is chill : the forest bare :
> Is it the wind that moaneth bleak ?
> There is not wind enough in the air
> To move away the ringlet curl
> From the lovely lady's cheek —
> There is not wind enough to twirl
> The one red leaf, the last of its clan,
> That dances as often as dance it can,
> Hanging so light, and hanging so high,
> On the topmost twig that looks up at the sky.

Note the effect imparted by the running on of the
three verses in reply to the question, ' Is it the wind
that moaneth bleak ? ' And then the effect of the
monosyllabic words in the verses that follow, their
staccato effect being heightened by the dissyllabic
words that add to the number of light syllables.

In every verse of 'Christabel,' the number of accents,
and, consequently, the number of feet, are regularly
four ; but the number of syllables varies from seven
to twelve, the *xa* rhythm being changed sometimes to
the *axx* or *xxa*. But the variation in the number of
syllables is not made arbitrarily or for the mere ends
of convenience, but in correspondence with some

transition in the nature of the imagery or passion.
The two following *ara* verses, descriptive of the
castle-gate, are admirably suggestive of the massive-
ness and strength of the gate, and of the image
of the bold knights on their spirited steeds, issuing
through it :

> The gate that was ironed within and without,
> Where an army in battle array had marched out.

The vowel melody of the following verses is most
suggestive :

> Outside her kennel, the mastiff old
> Lay fast asleep, in moonshine cold.
> The mastiff old did not awake,
> Yet she an angry moan did make!
> And what can ail the mastiff bitch?
> Never till now she uttered yell
> Beneath the eye of Christabel.
> Perhaps it is the owlet's scritch :
> For what can ail the mastiff bitch?

> Sweet Christabel her feet doth bare,
> And, jealous of the listening air,
> They steal their way from stair to stair,
> Now in glimmer, and now in gloom,
> And now they pass the Baron's room,
> As still as death with stifled breath'
> And now have reached her chamber door;
> And now doth Geraldine press down
> The rushes of the chamber floor
> The moonshine dim in the open air,
> And not a moonbeam enters here

> But they without its light can see
> The chamber carved so curiously,
> Carved with figures strange and sweet,
> All made out of the carver's brain,

For a lady's chamber meet :
The lamp with twofold silver chain
Is fastened to an angel's feet,
The silver lamp burns dead and dim ;
But Christabel the lamp will trim.
She trimmed the lamp, and made it bright,
And left it swinging to and fro,
While Geraldine in wretched plight
Sank down upon the floor below.

So much, for the present, in regard to the first two unities I have named, foot and verse, into which feeling moulds language ; and the enforcing and fusing or combining agencies of these, namely, accent and melody.

c. HARMONY AND RHYME.

The fusing and combining agencies of the stanza,[1] the third unity I have named, are, 1. Harmony ; 2. Rhyme.

We often meet with stanzas, the individual verses of which are sufficiently melodious, but all the verses when taken together, of which the stanzas are composed, are deficient in harmony, and consequently there is little or no fusion. The esemplastic power

---

[1] *Stanza* is exclusively applied to uniform groups of rhymed verses; but it can be with equal propriety applied to the varied groups of blank verses, as will be shown in the section on blank verse. For the proper appreciation of the individual verses in Milton's blank verse, they must be read in groups — a group sometimes beginning within a verse and ending within a verse. These groups are due to the unifying action of feeling, just as much as regular rhymed stanzas are; and, indeed, often more so. "The Italian called it *stanza*, as if we should say a resting-place." — PUTTENHAM, *Art of English Poesie*, ed. 1589, b. ii. c. 2. . . . "So named from the stop or halt at the end of it. . . . Cognate with English 'stand.'" — SKEAT's *Etymological Dictionary*.

of the writer's feeling was not strong enough, did not extend beyond the individual verse. In such case, a stanza is but an arbitrary group or succession of verses, and not a vital unity.

The second combining agency of the stanza I have named, is *Rhyme*.

(Rhyme is the likeness, with a difference, — unity in variety, — of final words of two or more verses. If they are monosyllabic words, their vowels and the consonants which follow them are alike (as pronounced, of course, not necessarily as spelled), while the consonants which precede them are unlike, the likeness and the unlikeness constituting a harmony : hills, rills ; hall, wall ; then, again ; mead, reed ; thought, caught ; banks, ranks ; chance, trance ; peers, years ; change, grange ; where two consonants precede, one may be common to both words, as breeze, freeze ; phrase, praise ; play, flay. The common letter is generally *l* or *r*. If the rhyming words are dissyllabic or trisyllabic, the vowels of their accented syllables, and the consonants or syllables which follow them, are in unison, while the consonants or syllables which precede them, are not : opinion, dominion ; docile, fossil ; rehearsal, universal ; allotted, besotted ; studied, bloodied.

Words pronounced alike, though they differ in spelling and signification, cannot be said to rhyme. They are simply identical. There is no variation to make a harmony. Such words as the following, for example : air, heir ; berry, bury ; cent, scent, sent ; cite, sight, site ; climb, clime ; cygnet, signet ; eye, I ; fain, feign, and numerous others.)

Rhyme is an agency which can be more easily employed than harmony, and it may be employed by a poet to cover a multitude of sins of melody and harmony. In writing blank verse, the poet has to depend upon the melodious movement of the individual verses, pause-melody, and the general harmony or toning. (It is only when a poet's feeling is all-embracing, is sufficiently sustained, that he can succeed in writing blank verse, with the fullest success.

Rhyme, while it is an important combining agency of the stanza, is also an enforcing agency of the individual verse. Hence, the second verse of a rhyming couplet must be slightly stronger than the first, in order to support the enforcement imparted by the rhyme. In humorous poetry, a ludicrous effect is often secured by the poet's advisedly making the verse on which rhyme falls, too weak to support it. Butler frequently does this in his ' Hudibras.' The rhyme emphasis of a verse is, of course, in proportion to the nearness of the verse to that with which it rhymes. If it is far separated from it, the emphasis will be more or less neutralized. In Collins's ' Ode on the Passions,' there are adjacent, alternate, and remote rhymes. Any one reading this Ode must feel the different degrees of the rhyme-emphasis, resulting from the different degrees of nearness or remoteness of the rhyming verses. In the first sixteen verses, the rhyming verses are adjacent, and one rhyme is a double rhyme (fainting, painting) :

When Music, heavenly maid, was young,
While yet in early Greece she sung.

The Passions oft, to hear her shell,
Thronged around her magic cell,
Exulting, trembling, raging, fainting,
Possest beyond the Muse's painting;
By turns they felt the glowing mind
Disturbed, delighted, raised, refined;
Till once, 'tis said, when all were fired,
Filled with fury, rapt, inspired,
From the supporting myrtles round
They snatched her instruments of sound;
And, as they oft had heard apart
Sweet lessons of her forceful art,
Each, for madness ruled the hour,
Would prove his own expressive power.

Then follow three quatrains, — the rhymes being alternate, — and in passing to them the reduction of the rhyme-emphasis is felt at once:

First Fear, his hand, its skill to try,
 Amid the chords bewildered laid,
And back recoiled, he knew not why,
 E'en at the sound himself had made.

Next Anger rushed; his eyes on fire
 In lightnings owned his secret stings;
In one rude clash he struck the lyre,
 And swept with hurried hand the strings.

With woful measures, wan Despair,
 Low sullen sounds, his grief beguiled,
A solemn, strange, and mingled air;
 'Twas sad by fits, by starts 'twas wild.

The next ten verses, twenty-ninth to thirty-eighth inclusive, descriptive of Hope, are particularly interesting, as illustrating rhyme-emphasis. The first and the tenth verses rhyme together, but they are so remote that the rhyme-emphasis on the tenth verse is quite neutralized. There are very few readers that would spontaneously retain the final sound of the first verse when they arrived at the final sound of the tenth. The second and third verses rhyme, and the rhyme is a double rhyme (measure, pleasure), and the emphasis is consequently strong. Then there are four verses rhyming alternately, the rhyme-emphasis being, in consequence, a little lighter; then the next two verses rhyme together, and the rhyme-emphasis is a little stronger again. The rhyme-scheme being *abbcdcdcca.*

> But thou, O Hope, with eyes so fair,
> What was thy delightful measure?
> Still it whispered promised pleasure,
> And bade the lovely scenes at distance hail !
> Still would her touch the strain prolong,
> And from the rocks, the woods, the vale,
> She called on Echo still thro' all the song :
> And, where her sweetest theme she chose,
> A soft responsive voice was heard at every close,
> And Hope enchanted smiled, and waved her golden hair.

The entire Ode affords an admirable study of this feature of Prosody, and also of the emphasis secured by the varied length of verses, about which I shall speak further on.

When a rhyme is repeated a number of times, the emphasis gathers up to a certain point. Beyond that, it would pester the ear, and lose its effect; in other words, it would be neutralized more or less by a monotonous iteration.

If the rhyme is double, the emphasis is, of course, still more marked. Mrs. Browning is fond of the

double rhyme, and employs it with great effect in
some of her shorter poems; in 'Cowper's Grave,'
for example:

It is a place where poets crowned may feel the heart's decaying,
It is a place where happy saints may weep amid their praying:
Yet let the grief and humbleness, as low as silence languish !
Earth surely now may give her calm to whom she gave her
    anguish.

O poets ! from a maniac's tongue was poured the deathless
    singing !
O Christians ! at your cross of hope, a hopeless hand was
    clinging !
O men ! this man in brotherhood your weary path beguiling,
Groaned inly while he taught you peace, and died while ye
    were smiling.

Robert Browning is a great master of rhyme ; and
his poetry abounds in every variety of rhyme-effect.
His poem 'Of Pacchiarotto, and how he worked in
Distemper,' and his 'Flight of the Duchess' afford
remarkable and surprising examples of double and
triple rhymes.

The English ear is not so accustomed to the double
rhyme as is the Italian ear, and the poet who employs
it in serious verse, must employ it with the best artistic
taste and judgment.   Its emphasis is too pronounced.
It is employed with the best effect, as an exceptional
rhyme, and for some special emphasis.   Byron so
employs it in his 'Don Juan,' as he does also the
triple rhyme, which is still more emphatic.

In all the more reckless stanzas of 'Don Juan,'
that is, when the poet plays with the feelings, often to
the extent of doing an irreverent violence to them, the

double rhyme comes out; when the tone softens, and becomes more serious, it is not employed to the same extent; it is sometimes not employed at all, often for a number of stanzas. In fact, the double and triple rhymes, throughout the poem, indicate a reduction of true poetic seriousness. Take, for example, a stanza like the following, descriptive of life, in ' Don Juan,' Canto xv. St. 99; its tone does not admit the double rhyme :

> Between two worlds life hovers like a star,
>   'Twixt night and morn, upon the horizon's verge.
> How little do we know that which we are !
>   How less what we may be ! The eternal surge
> Of time and tide rolls on, and bears afar
>   Our bubbles; as the old burst, new emerge,
> Lashed from the foam of ages : while the graves
> Of empires heave but like some passing waves.

Or take the three following stanzas descriptive of things sweet, Canto i. St. 123–125. There's a tenderness of sentiment in the first which excludes entirely the double rhyme, *as Byron uses it :*

> 'Tis sweet to hear the watch-dog's honest bark
> Bay deep-mouthed welcome as we draw near home ;
> 'Tis sweet to know there is an eye will mark
> Our coming, and look brighter when we come ;
> 'Tis sweet to be awakened by the lark,
> Or lulled by falling waters ; sweet the hum
> Of bees, the voice of girls, the song of birds,
> The lisp of children, and their earliest words.

But in the next stanza, the *general* tone is less serious, and it is especially marked by the double rhyme which crops out at the end :

Sweet is the vintage, when the showering grapes
    In Bacchanal profusion reel to earth,
Purple and gushing: sweet are our escapes
    From civic revelry to rural mirth;
Sweet to the miser are his glittering heaps,
    Sweet to the father is his first-born's birth,
Sweet is revenge — especially to *women*,
    Pillage to soldiers, prize-money to *seamen*.

In the next stanza, he carries the unseriousness still further, and it is still more marked by the double rhyme, the last one embracing two pairs of words:

Sweet is a legacy, and passing sweet
    The unexpected death of some old lady
Or gentleman of seventy years complete,
    Who've made 'us youth' wait too — too long already
For an estate, or cash, or country-seat,
    Still breaking, but with stamina so steady
That all the Israelites are fit to *mob its*
Next owner for their double-damn'd *post-obits*.

In the description of Don Juan's mother, in the First Canto, this unseriousness is carried to an extreme of recklessness, which is exhibited in frequent triple rhymes. The description extends over twenty stanzas or more. Take for example the following:

Her favorite science was the mathematical,
    Her noblest virtue was her magnanimity;
Her wit (she sometimes tried at wit) was Attic all,
    Her serious sayings darkened to sublimity;
In short, in all things she was fairly what I call
    A prodigy — her morning dress was dimity,
Her evening, silk or, in the summer, muslin,
    And other stuffs, with which I won't stay puzzling

Oh! she was perfect past all parallel —
   Of any modern female saint's comparison ;
So far above the cunning powers of hell,
   Her guardian angel had given up his garrison ;
Even her minutest motions went as well
   As those of the best time-piece made by Harrison :
In virtues nothing earthly could surpass her,
   Save thine 'incomparable oil,' Macassar!

'Tis pity learned virgins ever wed
   With persons of no sort of education,
Or gentlemen, who, though well born and bred,
   Grow tired of scientific conversation :
I don't choose to say much upon this head,
   I'm a plain man, and in a single station,
But — oh! ye lords of ladies *intellectual*,
   Inform us truly, have they not hen-*pecked you all?*

It will be found interesting, in reading ' Don Juan,'
to note the part played by the double and triple rhymes,
in indicating the lowering of the poetic key — the
reduction of true poetic seriousness. What might be
called the moral phases of the verse of ' Don Juan,'
are, throughout the entire poem, extremely interesting.

Some of Byron's most powerful writing is found in
' Don Juan'; some of his tenderest; and the possible
flexibility of the English language is often fully realized. But when he wrote this poem, his better nature
was more or less eclipsed; but wherever it asserts
itself, we feel its presence in the moulding of the
verse, as much as we do in the sentiments expressed.

From what has been said of the double and the
triple rhyme, as employed by Byron, in his ' Don
Juan,' it must not be inferred that these are the *peculiar* functions of these rhymes. They may serve to

emphasize the serious as well as the jocose. The stanzas quoted from Mrs. Browning's 'Cowper's Grave' show this. The form in which Hood's 'Bridge of Sighs' is cast, is worthy of notice, in this connection. The verse is *a.x.;* and to add to the liveliness of the expression, the rhymes are, in most cases, triple rhymes, as, 'unfortunate,' 'importunate'; 'tenderly,' 'slenderly'; 'scornfully,' 'mournfully'; 'brink of it,' 'think of it,' 'drink of it,' etc. Such a form might seem at first view to be very ill chosen. But every reader of sensibility must feel that the rhythm and the rhyme, in this case, serve as a most effective foil to the melancholy theme. It is not unlike the laughter of frenzied grief.

Shakespeare understood the enforcement secured through rhyme as fully as he did every other element of impassioned expression. He knew the effect of iterated rhyme, and knew, too, just how far it could be carried without self-neutralization.

In Titania's address to the Fairies in 'A Midsummer-Night's Dream,' 3. 1. 167–177, the same rhyme is repeated a number of times in successive verses, with a gathering emphasis which accords well with the enthusiasm of the speaker:

> Be kind and courteous to this gentleman ;
> Hop in his walks and gambol in his eyes ;
> Feed him with apricocks and dewberries,
> With purple grapes, green figs and mulberries ;
> The honey-bags steal from the humble-bees,
> And for night-tapers crop their waxen thighs,
> And light them at the fiery glow-worm's eyes,
> To have my love to bed and to arise ;

And pluck the wings from painted butterflies ·
To fan the moonbeams from his sleeping eyes :
Nod to him, elves, and do him courtesies.

A rhyme could hardly, under any circumstances, be repeated in successive verses beyond the extent to which it is repeated here, without losing its effect in the resultant monotony.

III.

EFFECTS PRODUCED BY EXCEPTIONAL AND VARIED METRES.

R ELATIVE effects are produced by variations of metre on the theme-metre.

These effects will be seen in some of the stanzas presented and analyzed further on, especially that of Milton's ode 'On the Morning of Christ's Nativity.'

Southey's long poem, 'The Curse of Kehama,' affords an abundance of material for the fullest study of this feature of verse-building.

There is, perhaps, no composition in the language which affords so much material within the same compass, as Wordsworth's Ode on the ' Intimations of Immortality from Recollections of Early Childhood.'

The several metres are felt, in the course of the reading of the Ode, to be organic — inseparable from what each is employed to express. The rhymes, too, with their varying degrees of emphasis, according to the nearness or remoteness, and the length, of the rhyming verses, are equally a part of the expression. Double rhymes occur with a notable appropriateness. The same may be said of the few exceptional feet which occur.

Of the 203 verses of which the Ode consists, 100 are 5 *xa*. This is the theme-metre of the Ode, from which the relative effects of the other metres are partly derived. (The feelings of the reader of English poetry get to be set, so to speak, to the pentameter measure, as in that measure the largest portion of English poetry is written ; and accordingly other measures derive some effect from that fact.)

In the theme-metre, generally, the more reflective portions of the Ode, its deeper tones, are expressed. The gladder notes come in the shorter metres.

Of the other metres, there are thirty-nine 4 *xa*, forty-four 3 *xa*, ten 2 *xa*, six 6 *xa*, one 7 *xa*, one 2 *xxa* + *x*, one *xxa*, *xa*, *xxa*, *xa*, and one 3 *xa*, *ax*, *xa*, the three last being

> And the children are culling,
>
> And the babe leaps up on the mother's arm : —
>
> Even more than when I tripped lightly as they.

Note the effect of the *ax* foot (lightly) in the last verse.

The third section of the Ode is especially to be noted for the effects which it exhibits of varied metre :

> Now, while the birds thus sing a joyous song,
>   And while the young lambs bound
>   As to the tabor's sound,
> To me alone there came a thought of grief :
> A timely utterance gave that thought relief,
>   And I again am strong :
> The cataracts blow their trumpets from the steep ;
> No more shall grief of mine the season wrong :
> I hear the echoes through the mountains throng,
> The winds come to me from the fields of Sleep,
>   And all the earth is gay :

> Land and sea
> Give themselves up to jollity,
> And with the heart of May
> Doth every beast keep holiday: —
> Thou child of Joy,
> Shout round me, let me hear thy shouts, thou happy shepherd
> boy!

After a play of varied metres, the theme-metre is maintained, as it should be, in the closing section, there being but two departures from it, one 2.va and one 6.va, each of which has a special function and is felt to be organic:

> And O, ye Fountains, Meadows, Hills, and Groves,
> Forebode not any severing of our loves!
> Yet in my heart of hearts I feel your might;
> I only have relinquished one delight
> To live beneath your more habitual sway.
> I love the Brooks which down their channels fret,
> Even more than when I tripped lightly as they;
> The innocent brightness of a new-born Day
> Is lovely yet:
> The Clouds that gather round the setting sun
> Do take a sober colouring from an eye
> That hath kept watch o'er man's mortality;
> Another race hath been, and other palms are won.
> Thanks to the human heart by which we live,
> Thanks to its tenderness, its joys, and fears,
> To me the meanest flower that blows can give
> Thoughts that do often lie too deep for tears.

Wordsworth never wrote any poem of which it can be more truly said than of his great Ode, 'Of the soul the body form doth take.' The student of verse should memorize it, and frequently repeat it, until the varied forms come out to his feelings.

IV.

EFFECTS SECURED BY A SHIFTING OF THE REGULAR ACCENT, AND BY ADDITIONAL UNACCENTED SYLLABLES.

AS this is an important feature in the most organic English verse, a feature through which some of the best metrical effects, both logical and æsthetic, are secured, it is worth while to introduce the subject with some of Dr. Johnson's condemnations of the variety which is essential to harmony, contained in his Essay on the Versification of Milton, to show, if for nothing else, how far opinions about verse, in the eighteenth century, went astray, in respect to this feature, as they did in respect to many others — in most others.

'The heroic measure of the English language,' says the Doctor, 'may be properly considered as pure or mixed. It is pure, when the accent rests upon every second syllable through the whole line. . . .

'The repetition of this sound or percussion at equal times is *the most complete harmony of which a single verse is capable*,[1] and should therefore be exactly kept in distichs, and generally in the last line of a paragraph, that the ear may rest *without any sense of imperfection*.

---

[1] The italics throughout the extract given are mine. — H. C.

'But to preserve the series of sounds untransposed in a long composition, is not only very difficult, but tiresome and disgusting; for we are soon wearied with the perpetual recurrence of the same cadence. Necessity has therefore enforced the mixed measure, in which some variation of the accents is allowed. This, though it *always injures the harmony of the line considered by itself*, yet compensates the loss by relieving us from the continual tyranny of the same sound; and makes us more sensible of the harmony of the pure measure.'

Here we see that some variation of the accents is allowed *as a relief*. The expressiveness of such variation is entirely ignored. A departure from the 'pure' is a necessary evil. The thing to be especially noted is, that verse is regarded as an end to itself.

The Doctor continues:

'Of these mixed numbers every poet affords us innumerable instances; and Milton seldom has two pure lines together, as will appear if any of his paragraphs be read with attention merely to the music.'

(Here the Doctor must be understood to mean that wherever Milton's verses are not 'pure,' their music is marred!)

He then quotes the following from 'Paradise Lost,' iv. 720–735:

Thus at their shady lodge arrived, both stood,
Both turned, and under open sky adored
The God that made both sky, air, earth, and heaven,
Which they beheld, the moon's resplendent globe,
And starry pole: Thou also mad'st the night,
Maker omnipotent, and thou the day,

Which we, in our appointed work employed
Have finished, happy in our mutual help
And mutual love, the crown of all our bliss
Ordain'd by thee; and this delicious place
For us too large, where thy abundance wants
Partakers, and uncropt falls to the ground.
But thou hast promised from us two a race
To fill the Earth, who shall with us extol
Thy goodness infinite, both when we wake,
And when we seek, as now, thy gift of sleep.

'In this passage it will be at first observed that all the lines are not equally harmonious; and upon a nearer examination it will be found that only the fifth and ninth lines are regular, and the rest are more or less licentious with respect to the accent. In some the accent is equally upon two syllables together, and in both strong. As

Thus at their shady lodge arrived, *both stood*,
Both turned, and under open sky adored
The God that made both sky, air, earth, and heaven.

'In others the accent is equally upon two syllables, but upon both weak :

a race
To fill the Earth, who shall with us extol
Thy goodness *infinite*, both when we wake,
And when we seek, as now, thy gift of sleep.

'In the first pair of syllables [of a verse] the accent may deviate from the rigor of exactness, *without any unpleasing diminution of harmony*, as may be observed in the lines already cited, and more remarkably in this :

Thou also mad'st the night,
Maker omnipotent, and thou the day.

The Doctor confounds harmony with uniformity, and does not at all recognize the fact that variety is as essential to harmony as is unity. But the most surprising thing is that he is entirely deaf to the special *expressiveness* of variety in verse.

He continues :

' But excepting in the first pair of syllables, which may be considered as arbitrary, a poet, who, not having the invention or knowledge of Milton, has more need to allure his audience by musical cadences, should seldom suffer more than one aberration from the rule in any single verse.'

This is equivalent to saying that a poet, not having the invention or knowledge of Milton, cannot *afford* to sacrifice music by admitting irregular accents — music, of course, according to the Doctor, depending on uniformity of accent, all deviations from uniformity marring the music, but being necessary, occasionally, as a blessed relief !

The Doctor has still further condemnation to pronounce upon the passage quoted :

' There are two lines in this passage more remarkably inharmonious :

> this delicious place
> For us too large, *where thy* abundance wants
> Partakers, and uncropt *falls to* the ground.

' Here the third pair of syllables in the first, and fourth pair in the second, verse, have their accents retrograde or inverted ; the first syllable being strong or acute, and the second weak. *The detriment, which .he measure suffers by this inversion of the accents,* is sometimes less perceptible, when the verses are carried one into another, but *is remarkably striking in this place, where the vicious verse concludes a period.'*

Now the ripple which makes the last verse ' vicious,'

> Partakers, and uncropt *falls to* the ground,

not only contributes to harmony, but imparts a peculiar expressiveness and suggestiveness to the verse.

To take up again the interrupted sentence : ' The detriment which the measure suffers by this inversion of the accents, is sometimes less perceptible, when the verses are carried one into another, . . . and is yet more offensive in rhyme, when we regularly attend to the flow of every single line. This will appear by reading a couplet, in which Cowley, an author not sufficiently studious of harmony, has committed the same fault :

> His harmless life
> Does with substantial blessedness, abound,
> And the soft wings of peace *cover* him round.

' In these *the law of metre is very grossly violated* by mingling combinations of sound directly opposite to each other, as Milton expresses it in his Sonnet to Henry Lawes, by *committing short and long,* and setting one part of the measure at variance with the rest. The ancients, who had a language more capable of variety than ours, had two kinds of verse ; the iambic, consisting of short and long syllables alternately, from which our heroic measure is derived ; and the trochaic, consisting in a like alternation of long and short. These were considered as opposites, and conveyed the contrary images of speed and slowness ; to confound them, therefore, as in these lines,

is to deviate from the established practice.   But,
where the senses are to judge, authority is not necessary ; the ear is sufficient to detect dissonance ; nor
should I have sought auxiliaries, on such an occasion,
against any name but that of Milton.'

All this is sufficiently dreary.   What a noble pair
of ears Johnson reveals in the whole passage quoted !

It does not appear in any of his criticisms that he
ever thought of verse as having an end beyond itself.
With him, the object of verse was not the expression
of impassioned and spiritualized thought, but to be —
verse !

He regarded English verse, which is accentual,
under the conditions of classical verse, which is quan-
titative — made so by its being recited, or chanted, in
time.   Quantity, in classical verse, is a fixed thing ;
a long syllable is invariably long, and equal to two
short ones ; and a short syllable is invariably short.
But in accentual verse, the same monosyllabic word
may be an accented (*i.e.* may receive the ictus), or
an unaccented syllable, in a verse — the word ' and,'
for example, which might be supposed to be always
an unaccented syllable :

> Each leaning on their elbows and their hips.
>
> — SHAKESPEARE'S *Venus and Adonis*, 44.

> Yet hath he been my captive and my slave.
>
> — *Id.* 101.

> So were he like him and by Venus' side.
>
> — *Id.* 180.

In the following verse, the same word, ' you,' is
accented and unaccented :

> You leave us : you will see the Rhine.
>
> — TENNYSON'S *I. M.* xcviii. 1.

So in the following passage from 'The Princess,'
the words 'fight' and 'strike' are each accented and
unaccented, in the same verse :

> yet whatsoever you do,
> Fight and fight well ; strike and strike home.   O dear
> Brothers, the woman's Angel guards you, etc.
>
> v. 399.

The 1st foot is *ax* ; the 2d, *xa* ; the 3d, *ax* ; the
4th, *xa*.

Even 'to' before the infinitive may receive the
ictus :

> That 'gainst thyself thou stick'st not to conspire.
> — SHAKESPEARE'S *Sonnet*, 10. 6.

In the very next verse it is unaccented :

> Seeking that beauteous roof to ruinate.

So much by way of introduction to the subject of
this chapter.

Spenser, sometimes, for a special enforcement,
either logical or æsthetic, introduces an *ax* foot into
his *xa* verse, where, by employing the same words,
in a slightly different order, he might have preserved
the regular *xa* movement — an evidence that the
ripple in the stream is not arbitrary, but responsive
to the poet's feeling.

Warton, in his 'Observations on the Faerie Queene,'
indicates how verses, in which such significant ripples
occur, can be made smooth or 'correct' according to
the notions of the school of criticism to which he and
Johnson belonged ; but the special enforcement secured by the ripple is then lost.

As an example of an effective exceptional foot, take the last of the following verses:

> At length they came into a forest wyde,
>   Whose hideous horror and sad trembling sownd,
> Full griesly seemd: Therein they long did ryde,
>   Yet tract of living creature none they fownd,
>   Save Beares, Lyons, and Buls, which romed them arownd.
>
> — 3. 1. 14.

'Lyons' is an *ax* foot, which could have been avoided by a transposition of the words 'Beares' and 'Lyons,' thus:

> Save Lyons, Beares, and Buls, which romed them arownd.

But the poet is presenting a picture of savage wildness, and his feeling caused him to break the equable flow of the verse by an inversion of the regular *xa* foot. Any one in reading the verse, first, as it is given in the 'Faerie Queene,' and then with the *xa* movement preserved, will feel at once how much more suggestive the former reading is, of the special pictorial effect aimed after, than is the latter.

In the last verse of the following stanza, the poet employs two *xxa*, instead of three *xa*, feet, and thus secures a strongly impassioned emphasis (the stanza expresses the lament of Una for the loss of her companion, the Red-Cross Knight, when she meets with the friendly lion):

> ' The Lyon, Lord of everie beast in field,'
>   Quoth she, ' his princely puissance doth abate,
> And mightie proud to humble weake does yield,
>   Forgetfull of the hungry rage, which late
> Him prickt, in pittie of my sad estate.

But he, *my* Lyon, and my noble Lord,
How does he find in cruell hart to hate
Her, that him loved, and ever most adord
As the God of my life? why hath he me abhord ?'

—i. 1. 3. 7.

The voice should pass lightly over 'As the' and 'of my,' and should utter the words 'God' and 'life' with a strong stress. The verse, too, with one exception, is composed of short monosyllabic words, and these contribute something to the effect.

(It will be found that strong passion is most effectively expressed through the monosyllabic words of the language; not only because such words are, for the most part, Anglo-Saxon, but because their *staccato* effect subserves well the abruptness of strong passion. Shakespeare understood the peculiar effectiveness of monosyllabic words. Of their use in his Dramas, for the expression of deep pathos, or the abruptness of anger, hate, and scorn, see examples in King Lear, 2. 4. 112–115, 187–189, 194, 195, 269, 270, 274–280, 283; 3. 2. 1, 66, 67, 72, 73; 4. 17–19, 20–22; 6. 113, 114; 7. 67–69; 4. 2. 30, 31; 6. 96–104, 143–146, 178–186; 7. 45–50, 54–56; 5. 3. 8–19, 23–26, 258–264; 306–312. King John, 4. 3. 95–100, 116–124. Merchant of Venice, 3. 3. 4–17. Richard III., 1. 3. 103–133. Julius Cæsar, 4. 3. 1–125.)[1]

In the sixth verse of the following passage from Tennyson's 'Morte d'Arthur,' an *xra* foot, ' in an arch,' is employed with fine effect. Sir Bedivere, at the command of King Arthur, throws Excalibur into the lake :

[1] See my ' Introduction to the Study of Shakespeare,' pp. 101–111.

Then quickly rose Sir Bedivere, and ran,
And, leaping down the ridges lightly, plunged
Among the bulrush-beds, and clutched the sword,
And strongly wheeled and threw it. The great brand
Made lightnings in the splendour of the moon,
And flashing round and round, and whirled *in an arch*,
Shot like a streamer of the northern morn,
Seen where the moving isles of winter shock
By night, with noises of the northern sea.
So flashed and fell the brand Excalibur.

The repetition of the word 'round,' in the verse, also imparts something to the effect.

The voice should move rapidly over 'in an' and make a wide upward interval on 'arch'; and then the exceptional ictus on the following word 'shot' adds to the effect.

In the third verse of the following passage from Milton's ' Paradise Lost ' (iii. 739–742) there are two *xx* feet — '-y an aëry wheel,' — which are especially effective. Satan, in the disguise of a stripling cherub, having been directed to Paradise by the Archangel Uriel,

Took leave; and toward the coast of earth beneath,
Down from the ecliptic, sped with hoped success,
Throws his steep flight in many *an aëry wheel*,
Nor stayed, till on Niphates' top he lights.

An effective emphasis is also secured through the initial *xx* feet, ' Down from ' and ' Throws his.' The movement of the verse could hardly be finer. And a lightsome repose is secured through the last three words, 'top he lights,' which is aided by the heavy word ' Niphates,' and even by the alliteration of the *t,* in '-tes' top.'

> that sea-beast
> Leviathian, which God of all his works
> Created hug*est that swim* the ocean stream.
>
> — *P. L.* i. 202.

Of the effective verse, 'Created hugest,' etc., effective because it labors in its movement, Dr. Bentley remarks, 'This verse has accents very absonous [!]. To smooth it, I take the rise from *v.* 196, ejecting the four lines intermediate:

> In bulk like that
> Leviathan, whom God the vastest made
> Of all the kinds that swim the ocean stream.'

Cowper, who appreciated the *morale* of Milton's verse better than the learned and audacious 'emendator,' says of this verse: 'The author, speaking of a vast creature, speaks in numbers suited to the subject, and gives his line a singular and strange movement, by inserting the word *hugest* where it may have the clumsiest effect. He might easily have said in smoother verse,

> Created hugest of the ocean stream,

but smoothness was not the thing to be consulted when the Leviathan was in question.'

Of the great fishes, Milton says, in the description of the fifth day's creations:

> part, huge of bulk,
> Wallowing unwieldy, enormous in their gait,
> Tempest the ocean.
>
> — *P. L.* vii. 411.

Hugeness and unwieldiness could hardly be better suggested than they are, first, by the character of the

words themselves, and, secondly, by the movement of
the verse, the first two feet of which are *a̱xx* and *xa̱x*;
or, the scansion might be,

wallow ing unwield y enorm ,

an *a̱x* and two *x̱xa* feet; 'unwieldy' should receive
the downward inflection, and should be followed by
a pause ; so that the word is in effect an *x̱a̱x*.

The initial word 'Tempest,' used as a verb, is in
itself most expressive ; and being *a̱x*, it is emphasized
by receiving an exceptional ictus.

Dr. Bentley does not suggest any mode of *smoothing*
these verses !

So he with difficulty and labour hard
Moved on, with difficulty and labour he.

— *P. L.* ii. 1021, 1022.

The fourth foot of each of these verses is an *x̱xa*
('-ty and la-'). A suggestion of struggle is imparted
by the exceptional feet which is helped by the repetition of the phrase, 'with difficulty and labour.'

Much of the perfection of the verse of the 'Paradise Lost,' both in respect to its music and its rhythmical movements, its pause-melody, and the melodious
distribution of emphasis, was due, no doubt, to some
extent, to Milton's blindness, which, in the first place,
must have rendered his ear more delicate than it would
otherwise have been (it was naturally fine and had
been highly cultivated in early life, through a study of
music), and which, in the second place, by its obliging
him to dictate his poem instead of writing it silently
with his own hand, must have been one cause why
the movement of the verse so admirably conforms to
its proper elocution.

Every appreciative reader of the 'Paradise Lost' must recognize 'the beautiful way the poet has of carrying on the thought from line to line, so that not only does each line satisfy the exactions of the ear, but we have a number of intervolved rings of harmony. Each joint of the passage, when it is cut, quivers with melody.'

Mr. Abbott, in the section of his 'Shakespearian Grammar' devoted to Prosody, starts with a statement which is apt to convey, which does convey, a very false notion; a notion, too, which Mr. Abbott himself appears to entertain. He says: 'The ordinary line in blank verse consists of five feet of two syllables each, the second syllable in each foot being accented.

We both | have fed | as well | and we | can both
Endure | the win | ter's cold | as well | as he.'
— *J. C.* 1. 2. 98, 99.

That's quite true. But what he next says involves a false idea: 'This line,' he says, 'is too monotonous and formal for frequent use. The metre is therefore varied,'—*therefore* varied, that is, to get rid of the monotony;—'sometimes (1) by changing the position of the accent, sometimes (2) by introducing trisyllabic and monosyllabic feet.' 'It would be a mistake,' he continues, 'to suppose that Shakespeare in his tragic metre introduces the trisyllabic or monosyllabic foot at random.' Certainly it would. A great metrical artist never does anything at random. 'Some sounds and collection of sounds,' Mr. Abbott continues, 'are peculiarly adapted for monosyllabic and trisyllabic feet.'

The last sentence indicates what he means when he says that 'it would be a mistake to suppose that

Shakespeare in his tragic metre introduces the trisyllabic or monosyllabic foot at random.' He means,
as he shows in the next sentence but one, that there
is a law of *slurring* or suppression, by which extra
light syllables are forced into, or got over, in the
enunciation of the verse. It is of course important,
at the outset, to determine this law; but it is not
particularly important in *itself*. Now, why is it important? It is important to determine it, in order to
determine what are, and what are not, *significant*
departures from the *even tenor* of the verse — *significant* departures — that is, departures with an emotional
or a logical meaning.

The true metrical artist, or the true artist of any
kind, never indulges in variety for variety's sake.
That Shakespeare was a great metrical artist will
hardly be disputed. And Alfred Tennyson is a great
metrical artist. One remarkable feature of his verse
is, the closeness with which the standard, the modulus
of the verse, is adhered to, while there is no special
motive for departing from it. When he does depart
from it, he secures a special, often signal, effect. All
metrical effects are to a great extent *relative* — and
relativity of effect depends, of course, upon having a
standard in the mind or the feelings. In other words,
there can be no variation of any kind without something to vary from. Now the more closely the poet
adheres to his standard, — to the even tenor (modulus)
of his verse, — so long as there is no *logical* nor *æsthetic*
motive for departing from it, the more effective do
his departures become when they *are* sufficiently
motived. All non-significant departures weaken the

significant ones.   In other words, all non-significant
departures weaken or obscure the standard to the
mind and the feelings.

'The same principle holds in reading.   A reader
must have a consciousness or sub-consciousness of a
dead level, or a pure monotony, by which or from
which to graduate all his departures; and it is only
by avoiding all non-significant departures that he
imparts to his hearer a consciousness or a sub-consciousness of his own standard.   If, as many ambitious
readers do, he indulge in variety for its own sake,
there is little or no relativity of vocal effect — there
is no vocal variety, properly speaking, but rather
vocal chaos.   *There should never be in reading a non-
significant departure from a pure monotony.*   But
elocution is understood by some readers, especially
professional readers, to mean cutting vocal capers, as
good penmanship is thought by professional writing-
masters to consist in an abundance of flourishes.
And so, in order to secure the best effects, there
should never be in verse non-significant departures
from the normal tenor of the verse.   And great
metrical artists do not make such departures.   The
normal tenor of the verse is presumed to represent
the normal tenor of the feeling which produces it.
And departures from that normal tenor represent, or
should represent, variations in the normal tenor of the
feeling.   Outside of the general law, as set forth in
Abbott's 'Grammar,' of the slurring or suppression of
extra light syllables, which do not go for anything in
the expression, an exceptional foot must result in
emphasis, whether intended or not, either logical or

emotional. And if the resultant emphasis is not called
for, the exceptional foot is a defect in the verse,
entirely due, it may be, to a want of metrical skill.
It is like a false note in music. But a great poet is
presumed to have metrical skill; and where ripples
occur in the stream of his verse, they will generally
be found to justify themselves as organic; *i.e.* they
are a part of the expression.

The slightest ripple in the flow of the verse is that
caused by an inversion of the normal *xa* foot; but, as
shown in the following examples, it has always a
more or less appreciable effect, generally as imparting a logical emphasis — an emphasis of an *idea*. It
should be added that when a verse begins with an
ax foot, the second accent is felt to be somewhat
stronger, from the fact that it is preceded by two
unaccented syllables; for example, in the following
verse from 'Romeo and Juliet' (5. 1. 70):

> Need and oppression starveth in thine eyes.

The stress upon the second syllable of 'oppression'
impresses as stronger by reason of the two preceding
unaccented syllables, 'and' and 'op-.' Again, *xxa*
and *axx* feet, if organic, more generally impart a
moral emphasis; that is, they are exponents of feeling. It should be added that exceptional feet are
more emphatic in what I call, in my 'Introduction to
the Study of Shakespeare,' the recitative (or metre-
bound) form of Shakespeare's verse, than they are
in the more spontaneous form, for the reason that in
the recitative form, the sense of rhythm and metre is
stronger.

V.

EXAMPLES OF ORGANIC VARIETY OF MEASURES.

IN the following verses from Shakespeare, the exceptional *ax*, *axx*, and *xxa* feet, while being elements of melody and harmony, by imparting variety to uniformity, result in emotional emphases, or, sometimes, logical emphases.

> *Cankered* with peace, to part your cankered hate :
> — *Romeo and Juliet*, 1. 1. 102.

The repetition of the word 'cankered' is also effective here.

> As is the bud *bit with* an envious worm.
> — *Id*. 1. 1. 157.

The alliteration 'bud bit,' and the abrupt word ' bit,' help the effect of the inversion.

> Love is a smoke raised with the fume of sighs ;
> Being purged, a fire *sparkling* in lovers' eyes ;
> Being vexed, a sea *nourished* with lovers' tears :
> — *Id*. 1. 1. 196-198

> *Gallop* apace, you *fiery footed* steeds,
> — *Id*. 3. 2. 1.

> That run*away's eyes* may wink, and Romeo
> *Leap to* these arms, untalked of and unseen.
> — *Id*. 3. 2. 6, 7.

> Some word there was, *worser* than Tybalt's death,
> — *Id*. 3. 2. 108.

By leaving earth ?   *Comfort* me, *counsel* me.

— Id. 3. 5. 200.

Oh, bid me leap, *rather* than marry Paris,

— Id. 4. 1. 77.

Give me, give me!   Oh, tell not me of fear !

— Id 4. 1. 121.

Green earthen pots, *bladders* and musty seeds,
Remnants of packthread and old cakes of roses,

— Id. 5. 1. 46, 47.

Art thou so base and full of wretchedness,
And fear'st to die? *famine* is in thy cheeks,
Need and oppression starveth in thine eyes,

— Id 5. 1. 68-70.

The obsequies that I for thee will keep
Nightly shall be to strew thy grave and weep.

— Id. 5. 3. 16, 17.

What cursed foot *wanders* this way to-night,

— Id. 5. 3. 19.

What, with a torch ? *muffle* me, night, awhile.

— Id. 5. 3. 21.

Thou detestáble maw, thou womb of death,
Gorged with the dearest morsel of the earth,

— Id. 5. 3. 45, 46.

Saint Francis be my speed ! how oft to-night
Have my old feet *stumbled* at graves ! Who's there ?

— Id. 5. 3. 121, 122.

Poison, I see, hath been his timeless end :

— Id. 5. 3. 162.

Pitiful sight ! here lies the county slain ;

— Id. 5. 3. 171

Go tell the prince : *run to* the Capulets ;

— Id. 5. 3. 177.

A post from Wales, *loaden* with heavy news ;

1 *Henry IV.* 1. 1. 37.

I will from henceforth rather be myself,
Mighty and to be feared, than my condition ;
Which hath been smooth as oil, *soft as* young down.

Id. 1. 3. 5-7.

Breathless and faint, *leaning* upon my sword,

— *Id.* 1. 3. 32.

Fresh as a bridegroom : and his chin new reaped

— *Id.* 1. 3. 34.

Zounds, I *will* speak of him ; and let my soul

— *Id.* 1. 3. 131.

An extra emphasis is secured, of course, when the logical emphasis does not, as here, correspond with the rhythmical ictus.

And on my face he turned an eye of death,
Trembling even at the name of Mortimer.

— *Id.* 1. 3. 144.

I know you wise, but yet no farther wise
Than Harry Percy's wife : *constant* you are,
But yet a woman :

— *Id.* 2. 3. 111.

Shakes the old beldame earth and topples down
Steeples and moss-grown towers.

— *Id.* 3. 1. 33.

Bait it like eagles having lately bathed ;
Glittering in golden coats, like images ;

— *Id.* 4. 1. 99, 100.

Wanton as youthful goats, *wild as* young bulls.

— *Id.* 4. 1. 103.

His cuisses on his thighs, *gallantly* armed,

— *Id.* 4. 1. 105.

So did our men, *heavy* in Hotspur's loss,

— 2 *Henry IV.* 1. 1. 121.

And in his flight,
Stumbling in fear, was took.

— *Id.* 1. 1. 131.

Coming to look on you, *thinking* you dead,

— *Id.* 4. 5. 156.

Question your royal thoughts, *make the* case yours ;

— *Id.* 5. 2. 91.

I know thee not, old man : *fall to* thy prayers ;

— *Id.* 5. 5. 51.

A kingdom for a stage, *princes* to act:
— *Henry V.*, Prologue, 3.

Carry them here and there; *jumping* o'er times,
— *Id.*, Prologue, 29.

Gently to hear, *kindly* to judge our play.
— *Id.*, Prologue, 34.

Never was such a sudden scholar made;
Never came reformation in a flood,
— *Id.* 1. 1. 32, 33.

Grew like the summer grass, *fastest* by night,
— *Id.* 1. 1. 65.

Be in their flowing cups *freshly* remembered.
— *Id.* 4. 3. 55.

Hopeless and helpless doth Ægeon wend,
— *Comedy of Errors*, 1. 1. 157.

Lightens my humour with his merry jests.
— *Id.* 1. 2. 21.

Are my discourses dull? *barren* my wit?
— *Id.* 2. 1. 91.

Of credit infinite, *highly* beloved,
— *Id.* 5. 1. 6.

And gazing in mine eyes, *feeling* my pulse,
— *Id.* 5. 1. 243.

Beauty provoketh thieves *sooner* than gold.
— *As You Like It*, 1. 3. 112.

Which, like the toad, *ugly* and venomous,
— *Id.* 2. 1. 13.

Finds tongues in trees, *books in* the running brooks,
Sermons in stones, and good in every thing.
— *Id.* 2. 1. 16, 17.

anon a careless herd
Full of the pasture, jumps along by him
— *Id.* 2. 1. 53.

Therefore my age is as a lusty winter,
Frosty but kindly:
— *Id.* 2. 3. 53.

Sighing like furnace, with a woeful ballad
— *Id.* 2. 7. 148.

Full of strange oaths and bearded like the pard,
Jealous in honour, *sudden* and quick in quarrel,
Seeking the bubble reputation
Even in the cannon's mouth.

—*Id.* 2. 7. 150-153.

But, mistress, know yourself: *down on* your knees,
And thank heaven, fasting, for a good man's love:

—*Id.* 3. 5. 57.

I should be still
Plucking the grass, to know where sits the wind;
Peering in maps for ports, and piers, and roads;

—*Merchant of Venice*, 1. 1. 18, 19.

My wind, *cooling* my broth,
Would blow me to an ague,

—*Id.* 1. 1. 22.

Why should a man, whose blood is warm within,
Sit like his grandsire cut in alabaster?
Sleep when he wakes, and creep into the jaundice
By being peevish?

—*Id.* 1. 1. 84, 85.

Pluck the young sucking cubs from the she-bear,

—*Id.* 2. 1. 29.

The patch is kind enough, but a huge feeder;
Snail-slow in profit,

—*Id.* 2. 5. 47.

The stress should be on 'Snail'; the two heavy words of which the first foot is composed, add to the effect of the idea.

The watery kingdom whose ambitious head
Spits in the face of heaven,

—*Id.* 2. 7. 45.

Fled with a Christian! O my Christian ducats!
Justice! the law! my ducats, and my daughter!

—*Id.* 2. 8. 16, 17.

Happy in this, she is not yet so old
But she may learn ; *happier* than this,
She is not bred so dull but she *can learn* ;
Happiest of all is that her gentle spirit
Commits itself to yours to be directed,

        — *Id.* 3. 2. 161–165

You loved, I loved for intermission.

        — *Id.* 3. 2. 201

Take then thy bond, *take thou* thy pound of flesh :

        — *Id.* 4. 1. 307.

    In such a night
Did pretty Jessica, like a little shrew,
Slander her love,

        — *Id.* 5. 1. 22.

Here will we sit, and let the sounds of music.
Creep in our ears :

        — *Id.* 5. 1. 56.

Fetching mad bounds, *bellowing* and neighing loud,

        Id. 5. 1. 73.

Come, Antony, and young Octavius come,
Revenge yourselves alone on Cassius!
For Cassius is aweary of the world :
Hated by one he loves ; *braved by* his brother,
Checked like a bondman ; all his faults observed,
Set in a note-book, learned and conned by rote,
To cast into my teeth. O, I could weep
My spirit from mine eyes! — There is my dagger,
And here my naked breast ; within, a heart
Dearer than Plutus' mine, *richer* than gold :

        — *Julius Cæsar,* 4. 3. 93–102.

EXAMPLES FROM TENNYSON'S 'PRINCESS.'

Some of the best examples are found in Tennyson's
'Princess' and 'Idylls of the King.' Every ripple
in his verse, caused by a shifting of the accent, or by
additional unaccented syllables, imparts a motived

logical or emotional emphasis.   Such emphasis is
often increased by an accompanying organic alliteration.   Various other interesting metrical effects are
exhibited in the following examples.

> *Brake with* a *b*last of trumpets from the gate.

> while the twangling violin
> *Struck up* with Soldier-lad*die, and* overhead,

The abrupt vowels and final abrupt consonants of
the initial words, ' Struck up,' aid the effect.

> *Petulant* she spoke, and at herself she laughed ;

The abrupt vowel and consonant in ' Pet-' aid the
effect of the initial *axx*.

> he started on his feet,
> *Tore the* King's letter, snowe*d* it *d*own, and ren*t*
> The wonder of the loom thro' *w*arp and *w*oof
> From *sk*irt to *sk*irt ;

> but ' No !'
> *Roared the r*ough King, ' you shall not ; we ourself
> Will crush her pretty maiden fancies *dead*
> In iron gauntlets : brea*k* the *c*ouncil u*p*.'

> We rode
> *Many* a *l*ong *l*eague back *to the North.*   At last

> There stood a bust of Pallas for a sign,
> By two sphere lamps *blazoned* like Heaven and Earth
> *With con*stellation and *with con*tinent,
> Above an entry :

> *D*rink *d*eep, until the habits of the slave,
> The sins of emptiness, *gossip* and spite
> And slander, die.

> She ended here, and beckoned us: the rest
> *Parted* ; and, glowing full-faced welcome, she
> Began to address us, and was moving on
> In gratulation, till as when a boat
> *Tacks, and* the slackened sail *flaps, all* her voice
> *Faltering* and *fluttering in* her throat, she cried,
> My brother.
>
> I would be that for ever which I seem
> *Woman*, if I might sit beside your feet,
>
>   elegies
> And quoted odes, and jewels five-words-long
> That on the stretched forefinger of all Time
> *Sparkle* for ever:

An extra effect is imparted to the effect of the *ax* foot, 'Sparkle,' by the additional light syllable '-er' of 'ever,' before the break.

>   I learnt more from her in a flash,
> Than if my brainpan were an empty hull,
> And every Muse *tumbled* a science in.

The abrupt word 'in' receiving the ictus, adds to the effect of the *ax* foot, 'tumbled.'

>   once or twice I thought to roar
> To *break* my *chain*, to *shake* my *mane*: but thou,
> *Modulate* me, Soul of *m*incing *m*i*m*icry!
>
> While the great organ almost burst his pipes,
> *Groaning* for power, and ro*lling* thro' the court
> A *long* me*lo*dious thunder to the *sound*
> Of *s*olemn psalms, and *s*ilver *lit*anies.
>
> There while we stood beside the fount, and watched
> Or seemed to watch the dan*cing bubble*, approached
> Melissa.

Here the exceptional foot is an *xax*.

> And up we came to where the river sloped
> To plunge in cat*aract, shattering on* black *b*locks
> A *b*readth of thunder.

>   we wound
> About the cliffs, the copses, out and in,
> *Hammering* and clinking, chat*tering stony* names
> Of shale and hornblend, rag and trap and tuff,
> Amygdaloid and trachyte, *till the Sun*
> *Grew broader toward his death and fell, and all*
> *The rosy heights came out above the lawns.*

Note with what beauty the italicized verses come
in after the ' stony names.'

> Then she ' Let some one sing to us : *lightlier m*ove
> The *m*inutes fledged with *m*usic : '

> So sweet a *v*oice and *v*ague, *fatal* to men,

> Not vassals to be beat, nor pretty babes
> *To be dan*dled, no, but living wills, and sphered
> Whole in ourselves and owed to none.

>   hoof by hoof,
> And every hoof a knell to my desires,
> *Clanged on* the bridge ;

> For blind rage she missed the plank, and rolled
> *In the riv*er.   Out I sprang from *g*low to *g*loom :
> There *whirl*ed her *wh*ite *r*obe *l*ike a *b*lossomed *b*ranch
> *Rapt to* the hor*rible fall :* a glance I gave,
> No more ; but woman vested as I was,
> *Plunged ; and* the flood drew ; yet I caught her ; then
> *Oaring* one arm, and bearing in my left
> The weight of all the hopes of half the world,
> *Strove to buffet* to land in vain.

The metrical effects of this passage are especially
notable.   Note effect of the *xxa* foot, ' In the riv-,'

coming in without a pause, after the prolongable word 'rolled'; the alliterations in the third verse; the initial *ax* feet of the fourth, sixth, and seventh verses; the very effective *xxa* foot, '-ribble fall,' in the fourth verse; the suggestion of struggle in the two *ax* feet of the last verse.

> A little space was left between the horns,
> Thro' which I clambered o'er at top with pain,
> *Dropt on* the sward, and *up* the linden walks.

Note, too, the effect of the abrupt words, 'Dropt' and 'up.'

> I heard the *puffed pursuer*; at mine ear
> *Bubbled* the nightingale and heeded not,
> And *secret laughter tickled all* my *soul*.

>   above her drooped a lamp,
> And made the single jewel on her *brow*
> *Burn like* the mystic fire on a mast-head,
> *Prophet* of storm.

>   and close behind her stood
> Eight daughters of the plough, *stronger* than men,

> As of some fire against a stormy cloud,
> When the wild peasant rights himself, the rick
> *Flames, and* his anger reddens in the heavens:

>   her breast,
> Beaten with some great passion at her heart,
> *Palpitated*, her hand shook, and we heard
> In the dead hush the papers that she held
> *Rustle:*

>   they to and fro
> *Fluctuated*, as flowers in storm, some red, some pale,

>   and the wild birds on the light
> *Dash themselves dead*.

Or, falling, protomartyr of our cause,
Die:

She, ending, waved her hands: thereat the crowd
Muttering, dissolved:

        While I listened, came
*On a sud*den the weird seizure and the doubt:

Breathing and sounding *b*eauteous *b*attle, comes
*With the air of the trum*pet round him, and leaps *in*
Among the women, snares them by the score,
Flattered and *f*lustered, wins, tho' *d*ashed with *d*eath
He reddens what he kisses:

        but other thoughts than Peace
Burnt in us, when we saw the embattled squares,
And squadrons of the Prince, *trampling* the flowers
With clamour: for among them rose a cry
As if to greet the King; they made a halt:
The horses yelled; they clashed their arms; the drum
Beat; *merrily-blow*ing shrilled the martial fife;
And in the blast and bray of the long horn
And serpent-throated bugle, undulat*ed*
The bann*er*: anon to meet us lightly pranced
Three captains out;

        and standing like a stately Pine
Set in a cataract on an island-crag,
When storm is on the heights, and right and left
Sucked from the dark heart of the long hills roll
The torrents, dashed *to the vale:*

        till a rout of saucy boys
Brake on us at our books, and marred our peace,
Masked like our maids, *blustering* I know not what
Of insolence and love.

        yet whatsoe'er you do,
Fight and fight well; *strike and* strike home. O dear
Brothers, the woman's Angel guards you,

                            and once more
The trumpet, and again ; at which the storm
Of *galloping hoofs* bare on the ridge of spears
And riders front to front.

The large blows rained, as here and everywhere
He rode the mellay, lord *of the ring*ing lists,
And all the plain, — brand, mace, and *shaft*, and *shield* —
Shocked, like an iron-clanging anvil banged
With hammers :

                            came
As comes a pillar of electric cloud,
Flaying the roofs and sucking up the drains,
And shad*owing down* the champain till it strikes
On a wood, and takes, and breaks, and cracks, and splits,
And twists the grain with such a roar that Earth
Reels, and the herdsmen cry ;

                            by them went
The enamoured air sighing, and on their curls
From the high tree the blossom wavering fell,
And over them the trem*ulous isles* of light
Slided, they moving under shade :

Thro' open field into the lists they wound
Timorously ;

Steps with a tender foot, *light as* on air,

                    Up started from my side
The old lion, glaring with his whelpless eye,
Silent ;

                    and when she saw
The haggard father's face, and reverend beard
Of grisly twine, all dabbled with the blood
Of his own son, *shuddered*, a twitch of pain
Tortured her mouth,

                        to them the doors gave way
Groaning.

And on they moved and gained the hall, and there
Rested:

                  she said
*Broken*ly, that she knew it, she had failed
In sweet humility;

The two-celled heart *beating*, with one full stroke,
Life.

The *ax* foot, 'beating,' gains additional effect
from the monosyllabic words before and after it.
The same is true of the preceding *ax* foot.

                the walls
Blackened about us, *b*ats wheeled and owls whooped.

Examples from the 'Idylls of the King.'

Gareth and Lynette.

      and Gareth loosed the stone
From off his neck, then in the mere beside
Tumbled it; oilily bubbled up the mere.

The last verse could hardly be more suggestive.
Its first two feet are, *axx* ('Tumbled it'), *ax* ('oili-'),
its third, fourth, and fifth are *xa*. If Milton had
written this verse, Dr. Bentley would no doubt have
pronounced it 'absonous'; and Dr. Johnson would
have said that 'the law of metre is very grossly violated by mingling combinations of sound directly
opposite to each other, . . . by committing short and
long, and setting one part of the measure at variance
with the rest.' Verily, 'the letter killeth, but the
spirit giveth life.'

And Gareth silent gazed upon the knight,
Who stood a moment, ere his horse was brought,
Glorying;

He spake; and all at fiery speed the two
Shocked on the central bridge, and either spear
Bent but not *brake,* and either knight at once,
Hurled as a stone from out *of a cata*pult
Beyond his horse's crupper and the bridge,
Fell, as if dead;

As if the flower,
That blows a globe of after arrowlets,
Ten thousand-fold had grown, *flashed the f*ierce *s*hield,
All sun;

Geraint and Enid.

And watch his mightful hand *striking* great blows

the pang
That makes a man, in the sweet face of her
Whom he loves most, *lonely* and miserable.

The Prince's blood *spirted* upon the scarf,
Dyeing it;

And out of town and valley came a noise
As of a *broad brook* o'er a shingly *bed*
Brawling.

The voice of Enid, Yniol's daughter, rang
Clear thro' the open casement of the Hall,
Singing;

and thrice
They clashed together, *and thrice* they brake their spears.
Then each, dishorsed and drawing, lashed at each
So often and with such blows, that all the crowd
Wondered,

But while the sun yet beat a dewy blade,
The sound of many *a heavily galloping hoof*
Smote on her ear, and turning round she saw
Dust, and the points of lances bicker in it.

And none spake word, but all sat down at once,
And ate with tumult in the naked hall,
Feeding like horses when you hear them feed;

He spoke: the brawny spearman let his cheek
Bulge with the unswallowed piece, and turning *stared;*

Merlin and Vivien.

And after that she set herself to gain
Him, the most famous man of all those times,
Merlin,

She took the helm and he the sail; the boat
Drove with a sudden wind across the *d*eeps,

But since you name yourself the summer fly,
I well could wish a cobweb for the gnat,
That *s*ettles, *b*eaten *b*ack, and *b*eaten *b*ack
Settles, till one could yield for weariness:

She ceased, and made her lithe arm round his neck
Tighten.

But Vivien, gathering somewhat of his mood.
And hearing ' harlot ' muttered twice or thrice,
Leapt from her session on his *l*ap, and *s*tood
Stiff as a viper frozen; loathsome sight,
How from the rosy *l*ips of *l*ife and *l*ove,
Flashed the bare-grinning skeleton of death!
White was her cheek: sharp breaths of anger puffed
Her fairy nostril out;

She mused a little, and then, clapt her hands
Together, with a wailing shriek, and said:
Stabbed through the heart's affections to the heart!
Seethed like a kid in its own mother's milk!
Killed with a word worse than a life of blows!

The initial *ax* in three successive verses imparts an
abrupt passionate emphasis to the speech.

And ever overhead
Bellowed the tempest, and the rotten branch
Snapt in the rushing of the *river-rain*
Above them: and in change of *glare* and *gloom*
Her eyes and neck *glittering* went and came;

Lancelot and Elaine.

And Arthur came, and labouring up the pass
All in a misty moonshine, unawares
Had trodden that crowned skeleton, and the skull
Brake from the nape, and turning on its rims
Fled like a *glittering rivulet* to the *tarn*:

    She watched their arms far-off
Sparkle, until they *dipt* below the *downs*.

A hermit, who had prayed, *laboured* and prayed

   and anon
The trumpets blew; and then did either side,
They that assailed, and they that held the lists,
Set lance in rest, strike spur, *suddenly* move,
Meet in the *midst*, and there so furiously
Shock, that a man far-off might well perceive,
If any man that day were left afield,
The hard earth shake, *and a low thunder* of arms.

They couched their spears and pricked their steeds and thus,
Their plumes driv'n backward by the wind they made
In moving, all together down upon him
Bare, as a wild wave in the *wide* North-sea,
Green-glimmering toward the summit, *bears*, with all
Its stormy crests that smoke against the skies,
Down on a bark, and over*bears* the *bark*,
And *him* that *helms* it, so they overbore
Sir Lancelot and his charger, and a spear
Down-glancing lamed the charger, and a spear

Pricked sharply his own cuirass, and the head
Pierced thro' his side, and there *snapt, and* remained.

       And all wearied of the quest
Leapt on his horse, and car*olling as* he went
A true-love ballad, lightly rode away.

Guinevere.

       aroused
Lancelot, who rushing outward *lion*li*ke*
Leapt on him, and *h*ur*led h*im *h*ead*l*ong, and *h*e fe*ll*
Stunned, and his creatures took and bore him off
And all was still:

       but she to Almesbury
Fled all night long by glimmering *w*aste and *w*eald,
And heard the Spirits of the *w*aste and *w*eald
Moan as she fled, or thought she heard them moan:
And in herself she moaned ' too late, too late!'
Till in the cold wind that foreruns the morn,
A blot in heaven, the Raven, flying high,
Croaked, and she thought ' he spies a field of death:'

And still at evenings on before his horse
The flick*ering fairy cir*cle wheeled and broke
Flying, and linked again, and wheeled and broke
Flying, for all the *l*and was *full of life.*

There rode an armed warrior to the doors.
A murmuring whisper thro' the nunnery ran,
Then on a sudden a cry, ' the King.'   She sat
Stiff-stricken, listen*i*ng:

  The alliteration and the repetition of the *I* in 'Stiff,'
'strick,' 'list,' '-ing,' aid the effect of the initial *ax*;
or to these perhaps is due the chief effect.

For perfect grace and an airy lightsomeness of movement; for melody and harmony, in all their various forms, from the most easily appreciable up to the most subtle; for organic variety of measures, such as is exhibited in the passages given above, and for almost every other element of poetic expressiveness, the young student can read no poems superior to the 'Idylls of the King,' — none that will serve better to tune his feelings to organic poetic form.

VI.

SOME OF TENNYSON'S STANZAS.

NO one can read, however superficially, the poetry of Tennyson, without feeling to some extent the adaptedness of his rhythms, metres, stanzas, rhyme-schemes, melody, harmony, and whatever else is embraced under the comprehensive idea of poetic form, to the theme and the entire spiritual motive. His forms are instinct with the indwelling spirit, and have grown out of it. 'Of the soul, the body form doth take.' 'Maud' is a treasure-house of organic poetic forms, Peter Bayne's opinion to the contrary, notwithstanding, that 'its music is the music of kettle-drums at a recruits' ball,' and that 'the poem in general will never be recognized as tuneful by the human ear.' The ever-varying rhythm, metre, and stanza, correspond with, symbolize, and incarnate the ever-varying subjective states and moods of the speaker, who is grief-fraught and 'perplexed in the extreme.'

The Stanza of ' In Memoriam.'

In the verse of 'In Memoriam,' instinct as it is with a sanctified sorrow, there

Is nothing sudden, nothing single:
Like two streams of incense free
From one censer, in one shrine,
Thought and motion mingle,
Mingle ever. Motions flow
To one another, even as tho'
They were modulated so
To an unheard melody.[1]

There is sweet music here that softer falls
Than petals from blown roses on the grass,
Or night-dews on still waters between walls
Of shadowy granite, in a gleaming pass:
Music that gentlier on the spirit lies,
Than tired eyelids upon tired eyes:
Music that brings sweet sleep down from the blissful skies.
Here are cool mosses deep,
And thro' the moss the ivies creep,
And in the stream the long-leaved flowers weep.[2]

An interesting study of rhyme-effect is afforded
by the stanza of 'In Memoriam.' Though the stanza
is not original with Tennyson (Ben Jonson having
employed it in an Elegy[3] in his 'Underwoods,' and
Dante Gabriel Rossetti, just before the 'In Memoriam' appeared, in 'My Sister's Sleep'), Tennyson
has made it peculiarly his own by the toning he has
imparted to it.

By the rhyme-scheme of the quatrain, the terminal
rhyme-emphasis of the stanza is reduced, the second
and third verses being the most closely braced by the

---

[1] 'Eleänore.'   [2] 'The Lotos-eaters.'
[3] In nine stanzas, beginning:

Though beauty be the mark of praise,
And yours, of whom I sing, be such
As not the world can praise too much,
Yet is't your virtue now I raise

rhyme. The stanza is thus admirably adapted to
that sweet continuity of flow, free from abrupt checks,
demanded by the spiritualized sorrow which it bears
along. Alternate rhyme would have wrought an
entire change in the tone of the poem. To be assured
of this, one should read, aloud, of course, all the
stanzas whose first and second, or third and fourth,
verses admit of being transposed without affecting
the sense. By such transposition, the rhymes are
made alternate, and the concluding rhymes more
emphatic. There are as many as ninety-one such
stanzas; and of these, there are thirteen of which
either the first and second, or third and fourth, verses
may be transposed without any violence done to the
sense. These stanzas should each be read, first as
they stand in the poem, and then with the first two,
or the last two, verses transposed.

The following stanzas admit of having their third
and fourth verses transposed.

> Old Yew, which graspest at the stones
>   That name the under-lying dead,
>   Thy fibres net the dreamless head,
> Thy roots are wrapt about the bones.
>
> — ii. 1.

> To-night the winds begin to rise
>   And roar from yonder dropping day:
>   The last red leaf is whirled away,
> The rooks are blown about the skies.
>
> — xv. 1.

> Still onward winds the dreary way;
>   I with it; for I long to prove
>   No lapse of moons can conquer Love,
> Whatever fickle tongues may say.
>
> — xxvi. 1.

Man, her last work, who seemed so fair,
　　Such splendid purpose in his eyes,
　　Who rolled the psalm to wintry skies,
Who built him fanes of fruitless prayer,

　　　　　　　　　　　　　— lvi. 3.

Who breaks his birth's invidious bar,
　　And grasps the skirts of happy chance,
　　And breasts the blows of circumstance,
And grapples with his evil star;

　　　　　　　　　　　　　— lxiv. 2.

And moving up from high to higher,
　　Becomes on Fortune's crowning slope
　　The pillar of a people's hope,
The centre of a world's desire;

　　　　　　　　　　　　　— lxiv. 4.

Yet feels, as in a pensive dream,
　　When all his active powers are still,
　　A distant dearness in the hill,
A secret sweetness in the stream,

　　　　　　　　　　　　　— lxiv. 5.

He reached the glory of a hand,
　　That seemed to touch it into leaf;
　　The voice was not the voice of grief,
The words were hard to understand.

　　　　　　　　　　　　　— lxix. 5.

Beside the river's wooded reach,
　　The fortress and the mountain ridge,
　　The cataract flashing from the bridge,
The breaker breaking on the beach.

　　　　　　　　　　　　　— lxxi. 4.

Bring orchis, bring the foxglove spire,
　　The little speedwell's darling blue,
　　Deep tulips dash'd with fiery dew,
Laburnums, dropping-wells of fire.

　　　　　　　　　　　　　— lxxxiii. 3.

Whereat we glanced from theme to theme,
　　Discussed the books to love or hate,
　　Or touched the changes of the state,
Or threaded some Socratic dream;

　　　　　　　　　　　　　— lxxxix. 9.

Ring out false pride in place and blood,
    The civic slander and the spite ;
    Ring in the love of truth and right,
Ring in the common love of good.

— cvi. 6.

See, also, Introductory poem, 4, 5 ; iii. 1 ; xvi. 5 ;
xx. 2 ; xxv. 2 ; xxviii. 3 ; xxxvii. 3 ; xxxviii. 3 ; xli. 1 ;
xliii. 1 ; xlix. 3 ; liii. 1 ; lxi. 2 ; lxiv. 6 ; lxvi. 4 ; lxix. 1 ;
lxxii. 6 ; lxxiv. 2 ; lxxviii. 3 ; lxxxiv. 5 ; lxxxv. 1, 9 ;
lxxxvii. 6 ; lxxxviii. 1 ; xc. 3 ; xci. 2 ; xciv. 3 ; c. 2 ;
cii. 3 ; cviii. 4 ; Concluding poem, 27.

The following stanzas admit of having their first
and second verses transposed:

I sometimes hold it half a sin
    To put in words the grief I feel ;
    For words, like Nature, half reveal
And half conceal the Soul within.

— v. 1.

And doubtful joys the father move,
    And tears are on the mother's face,
    As parting with a long embrace
She enters other realms of love :

— xl. 3.

From art, from nature, from the schools,
    Let random influences glance,
    Like light in many a shivered lance
That breaks about the dappled pools ;

— xlix. 1.

The mystic glory swims away ;
    From off my bed the moonlight dies ;
    And, closing eaves of wearied eyes,
I sleep till dusk is dipt in gray :

— lxvii. 3.

The yule-clog sparkled keen with frost,
    No wing of wind the region swept,
    But over all things brooding slept
The quiet sense of something lost.

—lxxviii. 2.

As in the winters left behind,
 Again our ancient games had place,
 The mimic picture's breathing grace,
And dance and song and hoodman-blind.

— lxxviii. 3.

At one dear knee we proffered vows,
 One lesson from one book we learned,
 Ere childhood's flaxen ringlet turned
To black and brown on kindred brows.

— lxxix. 4

Dip down upon the northern shore,
 O sweet new year delaying long:
 Thou doest expectant nature wrong;
Delaying long, delay no more.

— lxxxiii. 1.

See, also, Introductory poem, 3; i. 3; iii. 1; iv. 1, 4; viii. 5; ix. 4; xv. 2; xxx. 1; xxxiii. 3; lii. 2; lvi. 5; lxxiii. 2; lxxviii. 1; lxxx. 3; xcvi. 4; xcvii. 6; civ. 1; cxv. 2; cxxi. 2; cxxii. 5; cxxv. 1; cxxviii. 5; cxxx. 1; Concluding poem, 1.

The following stanzas admit of having either their first and second, or third and fourth, verses transposed:

I hear the noise about thy keel;
 I hear the bell struck in the night;
 I see the cabin-window bright;
I see the sailor at the wheel.

— x. 1.

I hold it true, whate'er befall;
 I feel it when I sorrow most;
 'Tis better to have loved and lost
Than never to have loved at all.

— xxvii. 4.

Whatever way my days decline,
 I felt and feel, tho' left alone,
 His being working in mine own,
The footsteps of his life in mine.

— lxxxv. 11.

See, also, x. i; xxxi. 3; lv. 2; lx. 3; lix. 3; lxxxv. 9; cvi. 2; cvi. 7; cxxviii. 4 ; cxxx. 3 ; cxxx. 4.

These stanzas should all be read aloud by the student, as they stand in the poem, and then with the first and second, or third and fourth, verses transposed as indicated. If he has any susceptibility whatever to rhyme-effect, he must feel the change wrought in the character of the stanzas by making their rhymes alternate.

The poem could not have laid hold of so many hearts as it has, had the rhymes been alternate, even if the thought-element had been the same. The atmosphere of the poem would not have served so well to conduct the indefinitely spiritual element which constitutes the essential life of the poem. The twelfth section affords a good illustration of the adaptedness of the stanza (due to the reduction of the terminal emphasis by means of the rhyme-scheme) to an uninterrupted flow of thought and feeling. The poet, in his impatience for the arrival of the vessel which is bearing the remains of his friend to England, represents himself as leaving the body, and hastening away, in spirit, 'o'er ocean-mirrors rounded large,' to meet it :

> Lo, as a dove when up she springs
>   To bear thro' Heaven a tale of woe,
>   Some dolorous message knit below
> The wild pulsation of her wings ;
>
> Like her I go: I cannot stay ;
>   I leave this mortal ark behind,
>   A weight of nerves without a mind,
> And leave the cliffs, and haste away

O'er ocean-mirrors rounded large,
　　And reach the glow of southern skies,
　　And see the sails at distance rise,
And linger weeping on the marge,

And saying, ' Comes he thus, my friend?
　　Is this the end of all my care?'
　　And circle moaning in the air :
' Is this the end?　Is this the end?'

And forward dart again, and play
　　About the prow, and back return
　　To where the body sits, and learn,
That I have been an hour away.

No other stanza, with a stronger terminal emphasis, could so æsthetically express the flight of eager desire, as it is expressed here.

A still more remarkable illustration of the peculiar adaptedness of the stanza is afforded by the eighty-sixth section.　The four stanzas of which it is composed constitute but one period, the sense being suspended till the close.　The rhyme-emphasis is so distributed that any one, hearing the poem read, would hardly be sensible of any the slightest checks in the continuous and even movement of the verse.

The poet addresses the sweet western evening air, after a shower, and invokes it to fan his brows, and blow the fever from his cheek, and sigh the full new life that feeds its breath, throughout his frame.　The poem, in its movement, is like a rhythmical zephyr. The reposeful ending on the final word ' Peace ' has a great charm :

Sweet after showers, ambrosial air,
　　That rollest from the gorgeous gloom
　　Of evening over brake and bloom
And meadow, slowly breathing bare

The round of space, and rapt below
　　Thro' all the dewy-tasselled wood,
　　And shadowing down the hornèd flood
In ripples, fan my brows and blow

The fever from my cheek, and sigh
　　The full new life that feeds thy breath
　　Throughout my frame, till Doubt and Death,
Ill brethren, let the fancy fly

From belt to belt of crimson seas
　　On leagues of odor streaming far,
　　To where in yonder orient star
A hundred spirits whisper ' Peace.'

The third verse of the 'In Memoriam' stanza receives a stronger rhyme-emphasis than the fourth, by reason of its rhyming with an adjacent verse; but in this eighty-sixth section that emphasis is somewhat reduced, by the very slight pause which is required, in reading, at the end of the third verse. In fact, no pause whatever is required there, in the first and second stanzas.

There is no other section of 'In Memoriam' in which the artistic motive of the stanza is so evident.

In reading this section, an equality of vocal movement should be preserved throughout. See, also, xv. st. 3–5; xcvi. st. 4–6; xcviii. st. 3–8; cxviii; cxxvii. st. 3–5 ; cxxxi.

The Stanza of 'The Two Voices.'

What the poet, in the 'In Memoriam' aimed to
avoid, in 'The Two Voices' he aimed to secure,
namely, a close emphasized stanza. The poem consists, in great part, of a succession of short, epigrammatic arguments, pro and con, to which the stanza is
well adapted. It is composed of three short verses —
4 *xa* — all rhyming together. The terminal rhyme-
emphasis, to which the shortness of the verses also
contributes, is accordingly strong, and imparts a very
distinct individuality to each and every stanza.

The following stanzas from the opening of the
poem, afford sufficient illustrations of the adaptedness
of the stanza to the theme :

> A still small voice spake unto me,
> 'Thou art so full of misery,
> Were it not better not to be?'
>
> Then to the still small voice I said :
> 'Let me not cast in endless shade
> What is so wonderfully made.'
>
> To which the voice did urge reply :
> 'To-day I saw the dragon-fly
> Come from the wells where he did lie.
>
> 'An inner impulse rent the veil
> Of his old husk : from head to tail
> Came out clear plates of sapphire mail.
>
> 'He dried his wings : like gauze they grew :
> Thro' crofts and pastures wet with dew
> A living flash of light he flew.'

I said, ' When first the world began,
Young Nature thro' five cycles ran,
And in the sixth she moulded man.

' She gave him mind, the lordliest
Proportion, and above the rest,
Dominion in the head and breast.'

Thereto the silent voice replied :
' Self-blinded are you by your pride :
Look up thro' night : the world is wide.

' This truth within thy mind rehearse,
That in a boundless universe
Is boundless better, boundless worse.

' Think you this mould of hopes and fears
Could find no statelier than his peers
In yonder hundred million spheres ? '

It spake, moreover, in my mind :
' Tho' thou wert scattered to the wind,
Yet is there plenty of the kind.'

Then did my response clearer fall :
' No compound of this earthly ball
Is like another, all in all.'

To which he answered scoffingly :
' Good soul! suppose I grant it thee,
Who'll weep for thy deficiency? '

The Stanza of 'The Palace of Art.'

In lines sent with the poem to a friend, the poet
calls it 'a sort of allegory' . . . of a soul,

A sinful soul possessed of many gifts, . . .
That did love Beauty only, (Beauty seen
In all varieties of mould and mind,)
And Knowledge for its Beauty ; or if Good.

Good only for its Beauty, seeing not
That Beauty, Good, and Knowledge, are three sisters
That dote upon each other, friends to man,
Living together under the same roof,
And never can be sundered without tears.
And he that shuts Love out, in turn shall be
Shut out from Love, and on her threshold lie
Howling in outer darkness. . . .

The lordly pleasure-house, the palace of art, which
this beauty-worshipping Soul built for herself, was,
she says, full of great rooms and small, all various,
each a perfect whole from living Nature, fit for every
mood and change of her still soul. Some were hung
with arras (tapestry), in which were inwoven land-
scapes, marine views, sacred, legendary, and mytho-
logical designs, etc.

These pictures constitute a prominent feature of
the poem; and it is evident that the poet adopted the
stanza employed by reason of its pictorial capabilities.
It is a close stanza, having an abrupt but, at the same
time, a strangely reposeful cadence. It consists of
four *ia* verses: the first is pentameter, the second,
tetrameter, the third, pentameter, again, and the
fourth, trimeter. The rhyme-scheme is *abab*. Now,
in quatrains, consisting of verses of equal length, the
rhymes being alternate, the rhyme-enforcement of
the third and the fourth verses, is about equal, unless
one of the rhymes be on a broader vowel than the
other. In the stanza before us the poet has secured
an extra enforcement of the final verse by making it
shorter by two feet than the first and third, and
shorter by one foot than the second. Its exceptional

length alone enforces it; and being shorter, the
rhyme-emphasis is increased, because the rhyming
words are brought closer together. It is felt that it
would not have served the poet's purpose to have
enforced it by making it longer than the other verses;
for a sweeping close would thus have been imparted
to the stanza, inconsistent with the repose of his
pictures, and with the general repose of the poem.

But to say thus much is to say very little indeed of
this remarkable stanza. The melody of individual
verses, the harmony which blends them into stanzas,
and the whole atmosphere of the poem, belong almost
exclusively to the domain of feeling, and are quite
beyond analysis. But the subtle adaptation of the
stanza to a pictorial purpose must be distinctly felt
by every susceptible reader. Tennyson has made it
forever as peculiarly his own as he has made the
stanza of 'In Memoriam.' No future poet, certainly,
will ever use them so organically.

'The stanza of "The Palace of Art,"' says Peter
Bayne, 'is novel, and it is only by degrees that its
exquisite adaptation to the style and thought of the
poem is perceived. The ear instinctively demands,
in the second and fourth lines, a body of sound not
much less than that of the first and third; but in
Tennyson's stanza, the fall in the fourth line is complete; the body of sound in the second and fourth
lines is not nearly sufficient to balance that in the
first and third; and the consequence is, that the ear
dwells on the alternate lines, especially on the fourth,
stopping there to listen to the whole verse, to gather
up its whole sound and sense. I do not know whether

Tennyson ever contemplated scientifically the effect
of this.   I should think it far more likely, and indica-
tive of far higher genius, that he did not.   But no
means could be conceived for setting forth, to such
advantage, those separate pictures, "each a perfect
whole," which constitute so great a portion of the
poem.'

The following are some of the picture-stanzas, 'each
a perfect whole':

> One seemed all dark and red — a tract of sand,
>   And some one pacing there alone,
> Who paced forever in a glimmering land,
>   Lit with a low large moon.
>
> One showed an iron coast and angry waves.
>   You seemed to hear them climb and fall
> And roar rock-thwarted under bellowing caves,
>   Beneath the windy wall.
>
> And one, a full-fed river winding slow
>   By herds upon an endless plain,
> The ragged rims of thunder brooding low,
>   With shadow-streaks of rain.
>
> And one, the reapers at their sultry toil.
>   In front they bound the sheaves.   Behind
> Were realms of upland, prodigal in oil,
>   And hoary to the wind.
>
> And one, a foreground black with stones and slags,
>   Beyond a line of heights, and higher
> All barred with long white cloud the scornful crags,
>   And highest, snow and fire.
>
> And one, an English home, — gray twilight poured
>   On dewy pastures, dewy trees,
> Softer than sleep — all things in order stored,
>   A haunt of ancient Peace.

. . . .

Or the maid-mother by a crucifix,
  In tracts of pasture sunny-warm,
Beneath branch-work of costly sardonyx
  Sat smiling, babe in arm.

Or in a clear-walled city on the sea,
  Near gilded organ-pipes, her hair
Wound with white roses. slept St. Cecily;
  An angel looked at her.

Or thronging all one porch of Paradise,
  A group of Houris bowed to see
The dying Islamite, with hands and eyes
  That said, we wait for thee.

Or Mythic Uther's deeply-wounded son [1]
  In some fair space of sloping greens
Lay, dozing in the vale of Avalon,
  And watched by weeping queens.

Or hollowing one hand against his ear,
  To list a footfall, ere he saw
The wood-nymph, stayed the Ausonian king [2] to hear
  Of wisdom and of law. [3]

Or over hills with peaky tops engrailed, [4]
  And many a tract of palm and rice,
The throne of Indian Cama [5] slowly sailed
  A summer fanned with spice.

Or sweet Europa's mantle blew unclasped
  From off her shoulder backward borne:
From one hand drooped a crocus: one hand grasped
  The mild bull's golden horn.

It is well known that Tennyson has been a deep student of the art of form and color. But if this

---

[1] King Arthur. [2] Numa Pompilius.
[3] *I.e.* from the Nymph Egeria. [4] Indented.
[5] The Hindu god of Love, son of Vischnu, represented as riding on the back of a parrot.

were not known, it would be naturally inferred by any appreciative reader of 'The Palace of Art.'

The student of verse should memorize these picture-stanzas, and often repeat them, if he would finally appreciate their subtler merits.

The Stanzas of 'The Daisy' and 'To Rev. F. D. Maurice.'

The stanzas of the two graceful little poems, 'The Daisy' and 'To the Rev. F. D. Maurice,' are interesting. The following are their first stanzas:

> O Love, what hours were thine and mine,
> In lands of palm and southern pine:
>   In lands of palm, of orange-blossom,
> Of olive, aloe, and maize and vine.

> Come, when no graver cares employ,
> God-father, come and see your boy:
>   Your presence will be sun in winter,
> Making the little one leap for joy.

The first three verses of each are 4 xa, the third verse having an additional light syllable. The rhyme-schemes are the same in both: the first, second, and fourth verses rhyme together. The third verse is non-rhyming. A strong rhyme-emphasis consequently falls on the last verse of each stanza, an emphasis not reduced by any other rhyme. The last verse of the stanza of 'The Daisy' is further enforced, and a playful effect is imparted to it, by the penultimate xra; and the enforcement of the last verse of the stanza of the other poem, and the playful effect, are carried still further, by its being composed of two

axx and an *axa* feet. The additional light syllable of
the third verse of the stanza of each poem impresses
as an anticipation of the rhythmical dance in the last
verse.

Tennyson always adheres very strictly to his verse-
schemes, whatever they are, and never departs from
them unless there be a very special emotional motive
for a departure. In these two poems there is no
departure whatever, and the skill shown in strictly
maintaining, throughout, the exceptional feet, in the
final verses of the stanzas, is admirable, especially in
those of the poem 'To the Rev. F. D. Maurice.'

The following are the final verses of the stanzas of
the latter poem. The two *axx* and the *axa* feet come
out in each with an apparent spontaneity:

> Making the little one leap for joy.
>
> Thunder ' Anathema,' friend at you.
>
> (Take it and come) to the Isle of Wight.
>
> Close to the ridge of a noble down.
>
> Garrulous under a roof of pine.
>
> Tumbles a breaker on chalk and sand.
>
> Glimmer away to the lonely deep.
>
> Emperor, Ottoman, which shall win.
>
> Dear to the man that is dear to God.
>
> Valor and charity more and more.
>
> Crocus, anemone, violet.
>
> Many and many a happy year.

For delicacy of sentiment and playful grace, ' The
Daisy' is unsurpassed. The beauty of the three

stanzas, which are somewhat of a higher strain, devoted to Milan Cathedral and the outlook from its
roofs, could hardly any further go. The brilliant
rhyme-vowel of the first stanza is very effective:

> O Milan, O the chanting quires,
> The giant windows' blazoned fires,
>   The height, the space, the gloom, the glory!
> A mount of marble, a hundred spires!
>
> I climbed the roofs at break of day;
> Sun-smitten Alps before me lay.
>   I stood among the silent statues,
> And statued pinnacles, mute as they.
>
> How faintly-flushed, how phantom-fair,
> Was Monte Rosa, hanging there
>   A thousand shadowy-pencilled valleys
> And snowy dells in a golden air.

VII.

THE SPENSERIAN STANZA.

THE Spenserian stanza calls for a special presentation and analysis, as it is one of the noblest of stanzas employed in English poetry, and includes within itself the greatest variety of the elements of poetic form.

No English poets have surpassed Spenser, in a melodious marshalling of words. The following stanzas, descriptive of the Bower of Bliss, have been frequently cited in illustration of this :

> Eftsoones they heard a most melodious sound,
>   Of all that mote delight a daintie eare,
> Such as attonce might not on living ground,
>   Save in this Paradise, be heard elsewhere :
> Right hard it was for wight which did it heare,
>   To read what manner musicke that mote bee ;
> For all that pleasing is to living eare
>   Was there consorted in one harmonee ;
>   Birdes, voices, instruments, windes, waters, all agree :
>
> The joyous birdes, shrouded in chearefull shade
>   Their notes unto the voice attempred sweet ;
> Th' Angelicall soft trembling voyces made
>   To th' instruments divine respondence meet ;
>   The silver sounding instruments did meet
> With the base murmure of the waters fall ;
>   The waters fall with difference discreet,

Now soft, now loud, unto the wind did call;
The gentle warbling wind low answered to all.

— 2. 12. 70, 71.[1]

As another example, take the following stanza
from the description of the abode of Morpheus:

And more to lulle him in his slumber soft,
  A trickling streame from high rock tumbling downe,
And ever-drizling raine upon the loft,
    Mixt with a murmuring winde, much like the sowne
    Of swarming Bees did cast him in a swowne.
No other noyse, nor peoples troublous cryes,
  As still are wont t' annoy the walled towne,
Might there be heard; but carelesse Quiet lyes
Wrapt in eternall silence farre from enimyes.

— 1. 1. 41.

The Spenserian stanza is composed of nine verses,
eight of them being 5.*ra*, or heroic, and the ninth 6.*ra*,
or an alexandrine. It has been common with Spenser's
critics to speak of his stanza as being the Italian *ottava
rima*, with the alexandrine added. John Hughes, who
edited Spenser's Works, with Life, etc., in 1715, says:
'As to the stanza in which the "Faerie Queene" is
written, though the author cannot be commended
for his choice of it [he does not tell us why], yet it
is much more harmonious in its kind than the heroic
verse of that age; it is almost the same with what
the Italians call their *ottava rima*, which is used
both by Ariosto and Tasso, but improved by Spenser,
with the addition of a line more in the close, of the

---

[1] In locating stanzas, quoted from the 'Faerie Queene,' the first
number will refer to the book, the second to the canto, and the third
number, or numbers, to the stanza or stanzas.

length of our alexandrines.' When he says 'it is almost the same with what the Italians call the *ottava rima*,' he means, as he himself shows, that it differs from it only in having the additional line. And Thomas Warton, in his 'Observations on the Faerie Queene,' says, 'Although Spenser's favorite, Chaucer, made use of the *ottava rima*, or stanza of eight lines, yet it seems probable that Spenser was principally induced to adopt it, with the addition of one line, from the practice of Ariosto and Tasso, the most fashionable poets of his age. But Spenser, in choosing this stanza, did not sufficiently consider the genius of the English language which does not easily fall into a frequent repetition of the same termination; a circumstance natural to the Italian, which deals largely in identical cadences.'

Here we have a number of misstatements. Both Hughes and Warton regarded the Spenserian stanza as the *ottava rima* of the Italian poets, with an extra line; and Warton makes the additional misstatement that the *ottava rima* was used by Chaucer. Now the eight verses to which Spenser added a ninth, are not the *ottava rima* at all, for the reason that they are differently bound together by the rhyme-scheme, and that makes all the difference in the world. We could as well say that any stanza consisting of four 4-*ra* verses, is the same as the stanza of Tennyson's 'In Memoriam.' In the *ottava rima* there are but two rhymes in the first six lines, the rhyme-scheme being : *ab ab ab cc*. Such a rhyme-scheme, especially in the Italian, with its great similarity of endings, is 'too monotonously iterative;' and the rhyming coup-

let at the close seems, as James Russell Lowell
expresses it, ' to put on the brakes with a jar.'

Fairfax employs the *ottava rima* in his translation
of Tasso's ' Jerusalem Delivered'; and great as is the
poetical merit of this translation, the reader soon tires
of the rhyme-scheme, the average resonance of which
is illustrated by the following stanza. Where the
vowels of the rhyming words are all bright or broad,
the resonance is still greater than in this stanza:

> Her cheeks on which this streaming nectar fell,
>   Stilled thro' the limbeck of her diamond eyes,
> The roses white and red resembled well,
>   Whereon the roary May-dew sprinkled lies,
> When the fair moon first blusheth from her cell,
>   And breatheth balm from opened Paradise ;
> Thus sighed, thus mourned, thus wept this lovely queen,
> And in each drop bathèd a grace unseen.
>
> — Bk. iv. 75.

It sometimes happens that the rhyme in the concluding couplet is on the same vowel as is one of the
rhymes in the sestet. In such case, the ear is still
more pestered with identity of sound. The following
stanzas, and there are many such, afford examples of
this:

> It was the time when 'gainst the breaking Day
>   Rebellious Night yet strove, and still repined ;
> For in the East appeared the Morning gray,
>   And yet some lamps in Jove's high Palace shined,
> When to Mount Olivet he took his way,
>   And saw (as round about his Eyes he twined)
> Night's shadows hence, from thence the Morning's shine,
> This bright, that dark ; that Earthly, this Divine.
>
> — Bk. xviii. st. 12.

Such as on Stages play, such as we see
  The Dryads painted, when wild Satyrs love,
Whose Arms half naked ; Locks untrussèd be,
  With Buskins lacèd on their Legs above,
And silken Robes tuckt short above their knee ;
  Such seemed the Silvian Daughters of this Grove,
Save that in stead of Shafts and Boughs of Tree,
She bore a Lute, a Harp, or Cittern she.
— Bk. xviii. st. 27.

In the last stanza, the rhyme of the concluding
couplet is a continuation (by chance, no doubt) of
the rhyme of verses 1, 3, and 5.ʹ There are many
other stanzas of this kind. But the poet, and not
the stanza, is here responsible.

The Epilogue to Milton's 'Lycidas' is strictly
fashioned after the *ottava rima* of the Italians, except
that the rhymes are not female rhymes. Such rhymes
would not suit the tone of the poem.

Thus sang the uncouth swain to the oaks and rills,
  While the still morn went out with sandals gray :
He touched the tender stops of various quills,[1]
  With eager thought warbling his Doric lay :[2]
And now the sun had stretched out all the hills,[3]
  And now was dropt into the western bay.
At last he rose and twitched his mantle blue :
To-morrow to fresh woods and pastures new.

The Elegy having come to an end, the *ottava rima*
is employed, with an admirable artistic effect, to mark

---

[1] In this lay ' the tender stops of various quills ' had been touched;
i.e. there had been changes of mood and minute changes of metre in
it (Masson).

[2] 'Doric lay': pastoral elegy; so called because the Greek pastoral
poets, Theocritus, Bion, and Moschus wrote in the Doric dialect.

[3] *i.e.* their shadows; 'majoresque cadunt altis de montibus umbræ'
(Virgil's *Ecl.* i. 84).

off the Epilogue in which Milton drops the character of a bereaved shepherd, and speaks in his own person.

Byron was fond of the *ottava rima*, and wrote in this stanza 'Don Juan' (1976 stanzas), 'Beppo' (99 stanzas), 'Morgante Maggiore' (86 stanzas), and the 'Vision of Judgment' (106 stanzas); in all, 2267 stanzas, comprising 18,136 *ava* pentameter verses. The demands which it makes on the rhyming capabilities of the language, he meets with a surprising facility. Those capabilities are more fully exhibited in 'Don Juan' than in any other production in English poetry.

To return to the Spenserian stanza :

If Spenser was indebted to any one for the eight lines of his stanza, he was indebted to his master Chaucer, who, in the 'Monk's Tale,' uses an eight-line stanza with a rhyme-scheme identical with that of the eight heroic lines of the Spenserian stanza, that scheme being *ababbcbc*.

Chaucer also uses this stanza in his 'ABC' (a Hymn to the Virgin), in 'L'Envoy de Chaucer à Bukton,' and in 'Ballade de Vilage sauns Peynture.' The Envoy to his 'Compleynte of a Loveres Lyfe' (or, the Complaint of the Black Knight) is also in this stanza.

The following is a stanza from the 'Monk's Tale,' according to the Ellesmere text :

> Allas, fortune! she that whylom was
> Dredful to kinges and to emperoures,
> Now gaureth [1] al the peple on hir, allas!
> And she that helmed was in starke stoures,[2]

---

[1] Gaureth: *gazeth.*   [2] Starke stoures: *severe contests.*

And wan by force tounes stronge and toures,
  Shal on hir heed now were a vitremyte;[1]
And she that bar the ceptre ful of floures
  Shal bere a distaf, hir cost for to quyte.[2]

By this rhyme-scheme, the couplet, instead of being at the end, is brought in the middle, where it serves to bind together the two quatrains. That is, in fact, what the eight verses are, namely, two quatrians, with the last line of the first and the first line of the second rhyming together. To these the poet added as a supplementary harmony, and in order to impart a fine sweeping close to his stanza, the alexandrine, making it rhyme with the second and fourth verses of the second quatrain.

James Russell Lowell, in his 'Essay on Spenser,' happily remarks, 'In the alexandrine, the melody of one stanza seems forever longing and feeling forward after that which is to follow. There is no ebb and flow in his metre more than on the shores of the Adriatic, but wave follows wave with equable gainings and recessions, the one sliding back in fluent music to be mingled with and carried forward by the next. In all this there is soothingness, indeed, but no slumberous monotony; for Spenser was no mere metrist, but a great composer. By the variety of his pauses — now at the close of the first or second foot, now of the third, and again of the fourth — he gives spirit and energy to a meas-

---

[1] Vitremyte: 'I suppose it to be a coined word, formed on the Latin *vitream mitram*, expressing, literally, a glass head-dress, in complete contrast to a strong helmet.' — SKEAT.

[2] Hir cost for to quyte: *to pay for her expenses.*

ure whose tendency it certainly is to become languorous. He knew how to make it rapid and passionate at need, . . .'

The following exposition of the rhyme-scheme addresses to the eye the evolution of the rhyme-emphasis, which culminates in the alexandrine:

1		*a*	6 .		*c*
2	.	. *b*	7		*b*
3		. *a*	8		*c*
4		. *b*	9		*c*
5		. *b*			

The rhyme which falls on the seventh verse is a third rhyme, with a resultant accumulated rhyme-emphasis; and the rhyme which falls on the alexandrine is a second rhyme, but the rhyme-emphasis is increased by reason of its being an adjacent rhyme. The alexandrine receives additional emphasis from its exceptional length. The poet, also, frequently, perhaps generally, imparts to it a special vowel and consonant melody, employs it for expressing whatever is lengthened out, or is of a continuous character, and renders it in various ways exceptionally vigorous.

The alexandrine of the following stanza affords a good illustration of this. (The poet compares the vile brood which issued from the maw of the monster Error, after the Red Cross Knight had slain her in her den, and which beset him on every side, to gnats molesting a shepherd, in the evening, while watching his flock.)

As gentle shepheard in sweete eventide,
　When ruddy Phebus gins to welke in west,
High on an hill, his flock to vewen wide,
　Markes which doe byte their hasty supper best;
　A cloud of cumbrous gnattes doe him molest,
All striving to infixe their feeble stinges,
　That from their noyance he no where can rest;
But with his clownish hands their tender wings
He brusheth oft, and oft doth mar their murmurings.

— I. I. 23.

To the regular enforcements received by the alexandrine from rhyme and extra length, are added those of alliteration and the most suggestive melody. First, there is the effect of the repetition of 'oft,' and the reversed order of the two verbs with the qualifying adverb (brusheth oft, and oft doth mar); then the transition from the vowel in 'mar,' through the vowel in 'their' ($= \breve{e} + \breve{u}$), to the two $\breve{u}$'s in 'murmurings,' which effect is heightened by the reduplication of the syllable 'mur':

He brusheth oft, and oft doth mar their murmurings.

The climacteric vowel is the broad *a* in 'mar,' which suggests the dash of the 'clownish hands,' into the 'cloud of cumbrous gnattes'; and the muffled cadence of the verse suggests their retreat. The entire stanza is a wonder of melody and harmony, culminating in the alexandrine.

Take it, for all in all, it is, perhaps, the most perfect stanza in the 'Faerie Queene.'

The following are good examples of alexandrines to which special enforcements have been imparted. The entire stanza to which each belongs should be read, in order to appreciate its full effect.

A streame of cole-black blood forth gushèd from her corse.
— 1. 1. 24.

Whose bridle rung with golden bels and bosses brave.
— 1. 2. 13.

adowne his courser's side
The red bloud trickling staind the way, as he did ride.
— 1. 2. 14.

the flashing fiër flies,
As from a forge, out of their burning shields;
And streames of purple bloud new die the verdant fields.
— 1. 2. 17.

He pluct a bough; out of whose rift there came
Smal drops of gory bloud, that trickled down the same.
— 1. 2. 30.

Whom all the people followe with great glee,
Shouting, and clapping all their hands on hight,
That all the ayre it fills, and flies to heaven bright.
— 1. 5. 16.

their bridles they would champ,
And trampling the fine element would fiercely ramp.
— 1. 5. 28.

High over hills and lowe adowne the dale,
She wandred many a wood, and measured many a vale.
— 1. 7. 28

Athwart his brest a bauldrick brave he wore,
That shind, like twinkling stars, with stones most pretious rare.
— 1. 7. 29.

Large streames of blood out of the truncked stock
Forth gushèd, like fresh water streame from riven rocke.
— 1. 8. 10.

The neighbor woods arownd with hollow murmur ring.
— 1. 8. 11

Who, all enraged with smart and frantick yre,
Came hurtling in full fiers, and forst the knight retire.
— 1. 8. 17.

Doth roll adowne the rocks and fall with fearefull drift.
— 1. 8. 22

They let her goe at will, and wander waies unknowne,
— 1. 8. 41.

And all about it wandring ghostes did wayle and howle.
— 1. 9. 33.

With mery note her lowd salutes the mounting larke.
— 1. 11. 51

So downe he fell, and like an heaped mountaine lay.
— 1. 11. 54

As fayre Diana in fresh somers day
Beholdes her nymphes enraunged in shady wood,
Some wrestle, some do run, some bathe in christall flood,

    — 1. 12. 7.

At last they heard a horne that shrillèd cleare
Throughout the wood that ecchoëd againe,
And made the forrest ring, as it would rive in twaine.

    — 2. 3. 20.

The mortall steele despiteously entayld
Deepe in their flesh, quite through the yron walles,
That a large purple streame adowne their giambeux [1] falles.

    — 2. 6. 29.

That is the river of Cocytus deepe,
In which full many soules do endlesse wayle and weepe.

    — 2. 7. 56.

That all the fields resounded with the ruefull cry.

    — 2. 8. 3.

He built by art upon the glassy See
A bridge of bras, whose sound hevens thunder seemed to bee.

    — 2. 10. 73.

They reard a most outrageous dreadfull yelling cry,

    — 2. 11. 17.

Like a great water flood, that tombling low
From the high mountaines, threates to overflow
With sudden fury all the fertile playne,
And the sad husbandman's long hope doth throw
Adowne the streame, and all his vowes make vayne ;
Nor bounds nor banks his headlong ruine may sustayne,

    — 2. 11. 18.

       the Boteman strayt
Held on his course with stayèd stedfastnesse,
Ne ever shroncke, ne ever sought to bayt
His tyrèd armes for toylesome wearinesse,
But with his oares did sweepe the watry wildernesse.

    — 2. 12. 29.

Till, sadly soucing on the sandy shore,
He tombled on an heape, and wallowd in his gore.

    — 3. 4. 16.

And in the midst a little river plaide
Emongst the pumy stones, which seemd to plaine
With gentle murmure that his cours they did restraine.

    — 3. 5. 39.

[1] Leggings, greaves.

Ne ever rests he in tranquillity,
The roring billowes beat his bowre so boystrously,
Like [1] a discoloured snake, whose hidden snares
Through the greene gras his long bright burnisht back declares,
                              — 3. 11. 28.
           his shield,
Which bore the Sunne brode blazèd in a golden field.
                               — 5. 3. 14.

Sometimes, but rarely, and chiefly in the later books, the poet uses double rhymes in the sixth, eighth, and ninth verses, and the rhyme-emphasis falling on the alexandrine is, in consequence, very much increased, as in the following examples :

So downe the cliffe the wretched Gyant tumbled ;
His battred ballances in peeces lay,
His timbred bones all broken rudely rumbled :
So was the high-aspyring with huge ruine humbled.
                               — 5. 2. 50.

There Marinell great deeds of armes did shew,
And through the thickest like a Lyon flew,
Rashing off helmes, and ryving plates asonder,
That every one his daunger did eschew :
So terribly his dreadfull strokes did thonder,
That all men stood amazed and at his might did wonder.
                               — 5. 3. 8

In the following it is still stronger, by reason of the broader vowel in the rhyming words :

Full many deeds of armes that day were donne,
And many knights unhorst, and many wounded,
As fortune fell ; yet little lost or wonne ;
But all that day the greatest prayse redounded
To Marinell, whose name the Heralds loud resounded.
                               — 5. 3. 6.

Such rhyme-emphasis, such a ' volée de resonnance,' is too stunning, and could not be borne very long.

       [1] Ed. 1596; Like to a (ed. 1590).

See, also, 5. 3. 9; 5. 4. 10; 5. 4. 15; 5. 5. 37; 5. 5. 40; 5. 6. 14; 5. 7. 29; 5. 7. 32; 5. 7. 42; 5. 8. 7; 5. 9. 9; 5. 9. 10; 5. 9. 24; 5. 10. 7; 5. 11. 50.

Attention should be called to another point in the passage quoted from Warton. He says : 'Spenser, in choosing this stanza, did not sufficiently consider the genius of the English language, which does not easily fall into a frequent repetition of the same termination ; a circumstance natural to the Italian, which deals largely in identical cadences.' To this objection it may be replied, in the words of Beattie, that the English language, 'from its irregularity of inflection, and number of monosyllables, abounds in diversified terminations, and consequently renders our poetry susceptible of an endless variety of legitimate rhymes.' In Italian poetry, the great majority of the rhymes are *female* rhymes, that is, rhymes in which two syllables, an accented and an unaccented one, correspond at the end of each line. The unaccented syllable will sometimes be *o* all through the stanza, sometimes *a*, sometimes *e*, sometimes *i*. The consequence is, that the ear, the English ear, at any rate, is terribly pestered by a constant recurrence of the same sound. For example, here are the rhymes of the first five stanzas of the first canto of the 'Orlando Furioso' of Ariosto :

amori, mori, furori; canto, tanto, vanto; Trojano, Romano.

tratto, matto, fatto; rima, prima, lima ; concesso, promesso.

prole, vuole, parole ; nostro, vostro, inchiostro ; sono, dono.

evoi, voi, suoi; apparecchio, vecchio, orecchio;
poco, loco.

innamorato, lasciato, tornato; lei, trofei, Pirenei;
Lamagna, campagna.

Christopher North takes Warton up on the opinion
quoted, in his characteristic way: 'A language,' he
says, 'like the Italian, so open that you cannot speak
it without rhyming, is the very worst of all — for
rhymes should not come till they are sought — if
they do, they give no pleasurable touch — " no gentle
shock of mild surprise " — but, like intrusive fools,
keep jingling their caps and bells in your ears, if not
to your indifference, to your great disgust — and you
wish they were all dead. Not so with the fine, bold,
stern, muscular, masculine, firm-knit, and heroic language of England. Let no poet dare to complain of
the poverty of its words, in what Warton calls "identical cadences." The music of their endings is magnificent, and it is infinite. And we conclude with
flinging in the teeth of the sciolist, who is prating
perhaps of the superiority of the German, a copy,
bound in calf-skin, of Walker's Rhyming Dictionary,
for the shade of Spenser might frown while it smiled,
were we to knock the blockhead down with our vel-
lum volume of the "Faerie Queene."'

THE PICTORIAL ADAPTEDNESS OF THE SPENSERIAN STANZA.

From the strong individuality of the stanza, due to
its compact and well-braced structure, and its fine,
sweeping close, we might decide, *a priori*, as to its

signal adaptedness to elaborate pictorial effect; and this adaptedness the reader of the 'Faerie Queene' soon comes to feel.

A great gallery of pictures, running through a wide gamut of coloring and tone, many of them possessing a satisfying unity within the limits of a single stanza, might be collected from the 'Faerie Queene.'

In 'Observations, Anecdotes, and Characters, of Books and Men: by the Rev. Joseph Spence,' Pope is represented as saying: 'After my reading a Canto of Spenser two or three days ago to an old lady between seventy and eighty, she said that I had been showing her a collection of pictures. She said very right; and I know not how it is, but there is something in Spenser that pleases one as strongly in one's old age as it did in one's youth. I read the "Faerie Queene" when I was about twelve, with a vast deal of delight; and I think it gave me as much when I read it over about a year or two ago.' (Ed. of 1820, pp. 86, 87.)

'The true use of him is as a gallery of pictures which we visit as the mood takes us, and where we spend an hour or two at a time, long enough to sweeten our perceptions, not so long as to cloy them. . . . as at Venice you swim in a gondola from Gian Bellini to Titian, and from Titian to Tintoret, so in him, where other cheer is wanting, the gentle sway of his measure, like the rhythmical impulse of the oar, floats you lullingly along from picture to picture.' — JAMES RUSSELL LOWELL.

A fine illustration of pictorial effect, to which the structure of the stanza contributes, is the description

of Prince Arthur, 'in complete steel,' in whom the
poet meant should be embodied all the several virtues
represented by the several knights. 'In the person
of Prince Arthur,' he says, in his letter to Sir Walter
Raleigh, 'I set forth magnificence in particular;
which virtue, for that . . . it is the perfection of all
the rest, and containeth in it them all, therefore in the
whole course I mention the deeds of Arthur applyable
to that virtue which I write of in that book.'

The forsaken and disconsolate Una wanders many
a wood, and measures many a vale, in search of her
long-lost knight, from whom she has been separated
by the wiles of Archimago.

> At last she chaunced, by good hap, to meet
> A goodly knight, faire marching by the way,
> Together with his Squyre, arrayed meet:
> His glitterand armour shined far away,
> Like glauncing light of Phœbus brightest ray;
> From top to toe no place appeared bare,
> That deadly dint of steel endanger may.
> Athwart his breast a bauldrick brave he ware,
> That shind, like twinkling stars, with stones most
> pretious rare.

The alexandrine glistens like the baldrick it describes.

> And in the midst thereof one pretious stone
> Of wondrous worth, and eke of wondrous mights,
> Shapt like a Ladies head, exceeding shone,
> Like Hesperus emongst the lesser lights,
> And strove for to amaze the weaker sights:
> Thereby his mortal blade full comely hong
> In yvory sheath, ycarv'd with curious slights,
> Whose hilts were burnisht gold, and handle strong
> Of mother perle; and buckled with a golden tong.

His haughtie Helmet, horrid all with gold,
Both glorious brightness and great terror bredd:
For all the crest a Dragon did enfold
With greedie pawes, and over all did spredd
His golden winges: his dreadfull hideous hedd,
Close couchèd on the bever, seemed to throw
From flaming mouth bright sparckles fiery redd,
That suddeine horrour to faint hearts did show;
And scaly tayle was stretcht adowne his back full low.

Upon the top of all his lofty crest,
A bounch of heares discolourd diversely,
With sprincled pearle and gold full richly drest,
Did shake, and seemd to daunce for jollity,
Like to an almond tree ymounted hie
On top of greene Selinis all alone,
With blossoms brave bedecked daintily:
Whose tender locks do tremble every one
At everie little breath that under heaven is blowne.

—1. 7. 29-32.

A rhythmical zephyr creeps through the last two verses.

Here is a pretty little picture of a hermitage and a chapel, in a dale, on the skirts of a forest, that may be hung under the larger picture of Prince Arthur. It is a picture of which all the elements mingle in one sweet impression:

A little lowly Hermitage it was,
Downe in a dale, hard by a forests side,
Far from resort of people that did pas
In traveill to and fro: a little wyde
There was an holy chappell edifyde,
Wherein the Hermite dewly wont to say
His holy thinges each morne and eventyde:
Thereby a christall streame did gently play,
Which from a sacred fountaine wellèd forth alway.

—1. 1. 34.

Observe how the 'crystal stream' flows through the alexandrine. And the alliterations, unobtrusive as they are, contribute not a little to the melodious and harmonious blending of the features of the picture: '*little lowly*,' '*down* in a *dale*,' '*far from* resort *of* people,' '*travel to*,' '*crystal stream*'; in the last verse there is an effective alternate alliteration of *f* and *w*, '*fountain welled forth alway*.'

Leigh Hunt, in his 'Imagination and Fancy,' presents 'A Gallery of Pictures from Spenser,' to each of which he has attached its character, and the name of the painter of whose genius it reminded him.

For these pictures, the student must turn to the 'Faerie Queene.' As given by Hunt, their subjects, characters, and the painters they suggest are:

Charissa; or, Charity. Character, Spiritual Love; painter, Raphael. (1. 10. 30, 31.)

Hope. Character, Sweetness, without Devotedness; painter, Correggio. (3. 12. 13.)

Marriage Procession of the Thames and Medway. Character, Genial Strength, Grace, and Luxury; painter, Raphael. (4. 11. 11, 12.) Arion. (4. 11. 23.)

Sir Guyon binding Furor. Character, Superhuman Energy and Rage; painter, Michael Angelo. (2. 4. 14, 15.)

Una (or Faith in Distress). Character, Loving and Sorrowful Purity glorified. (May I say, that I think it would take Raphael and Correggio united to paint this, on account of the exquisite *chiaro-scuro?* Or might not the painter of the Magdalen have it all to himself?) (1. 3. 3–7.)

Night and the Witch Duessa, taking Sansjoy in their chariot to Æsculapius to be restored to life. Character, Dreariness of Scene; Horridness of Aspect and Wicked Beauty, side by side; painter, Julio Romano. (1. 5. 28–32.)

Venus in search of Cupid, coming to Diana. Character, Contrast of Impassioned and Unimpassioned Beauty — cold and warm colors mixed; painter, Titian. (3. 6. 17–19.)

May. Character, Budding Beauty in male and female; Animal Passion; Luminous vernal coloring; painter, Titian. (7. 7. 34.)

An Angel, with a Pilgrim and a fainting Knight. Character, Active Superhuman Beauty, with the finest coloring and contrast; painter, Titian. (2. 8. 3–5.)

Aurora and Tithonus. Character, Young and Genial Beauty, contrasted with Age, — the accessories full of the mixed warmth and chillness of morning; painter, Guido. (1. 11. 51.)

The Cave of Despair. Character, Savage and Forlorn Scenery, occupied by Squalid Misery; painter, Salvator Rosa. (1. 9. 33–36.)

A Knight in bright armor looking into a Cave. Character, A deep effect of *chiaro-scuro*, making deformity visible; painter, Rembrandt. (1. 1. 14.)

Malbecco sees Hellenore dancing with the Satyrs. Character, Luxurious Abandonment to Mirth; painter, Nicholas Poussin. (3. 10. 44, 45.)

Landscape, with Damsels conveying a wounded Squire on his Horse. Character, Select Southern Elegance, with an intimation of fine architecture;

painter, Claude. (Yet 'mighty' woods hardly belong to him.)   (3. 5. 39, 40.)

The Nymphs and Graces dancing to a shepherd's
pipe; or, Apotheosis of a Poet's Mistress. Character, Nakedness without Impudency; Multitudinous
and Innocent Delight; Exaltation of the principal
person from circumstances, rather than her own
ideality; painter, Albano.   (6. 10. 10–12, 15, 16.)

Whoever reads these selections, however little
susceptibility he may have to organic literary form,
can hardly fail to be sensible, to some extent, of
the adaptedness of the stanza to the pictorial effect.
Certainly no other structure of stanza would contribute so much to this effect.   And the roominess
of the stanza allows of a detailed working-up of a
picture.   To tune the sensibilities to the subtlest
elements of poetic form, one need not go outside of
the wide domain of the 'Faerie Queene.'

In the Preface to his 'Fables, Ancient and Modern, translated into Verse from Homer, Ovid, Boccac-
cio, and Chaucer,' John Dryden says, 'We must
be children before we grow men.   There was an En-
nius, and in process of time a Lucilius, and a Lucre-
tius, before Virgil and Horace : even after Chaucer
there was a Spenser, a Harrington, a Fairfax, before
Waller and Denham were in being : *and our numbers were in their nonage till these last appeared.*'!
And in his Dedication of 'The Rival Ladies' to
Lord Orrery, he says : 'But the excellence and dig-
nity of rhyme *were never fully known till Mr. Waller
taught it;* he first made writing easily an art, first
showed us to conclude the sense, most commonly

in distichs, which in the verse of those before him runs on for so many lines together, that the reader is out of breath to overtake it. This sweetness of Mr. Waller's lyric poesy was afterwards followed in the epic by Sir John Denham in his 'Cooper's Hill,' a poem which, *for the majesty of the style, is and ever will be the exact standard of good writing.'!*

Verily, John Dryden perpetrated more rhetorical nonsense than any other literary critic that ever lived.[1]

[1] 'It was a firm belief of the writers of the period [of the Restoration] that then for the first time was the art of correct English versification exemplified and appreciated. It was, we say, a firm belief of the time, and indeed it has been a common-place of criticism ever since, that Edmund Waller was the first poet who wrote smooth and accurate verse, that in this he was followed by Sir John Denham, and that these two men were reformers of English metre. "Well-placing of words, for the sweetness of pronunciation, was not known till Mr. Waller introduced it," is a deliberate statement of Dryden himself, meant to apply especially to verse. Here, again, we have to separate a matter of fact from a matter of doctrine. To aver, with such specimens of older English verse before us as the works of Chaucer and Spenser, and the minor poems of Milton, that it was Waller or any other petty writer of the Restoration that first taught us sweetness, or smoothness, or even correctness of verse, is so ridiculous that the currency of such a notion can only be accounted for by the servility with which small critics go on repeating whatever any one big critic has said. That Waller and Denham, however, did set the example of something new in the manner of English versification, — which "something" Dryden, Pope, and other poets who afterwards adopted it, regarded as an improvement, — needs not be doubted. For us it is sufficient in the meantime to recognise the change as an attempt after greater neatness of mechanical structure, leaving open the question whether it was a change for the better.' — *Dryden, and the Literature of the Restoration*, by DAVID MASSON.

VIII.

THE SPENSERIAN STANZA AS EMPLOYED BY SUBSEQUENT POETS.

THE many great English poets who have employed the Spenserian stanza bear witness to the estimation in which it has been held. But in no other poet do we find the peculiar music which an educated ear enjoys everywhere in Spenser. 'The harmonies interwoven through the whole stanza, and each line elaborated with reference to the whole, the meaning and the music being incomplete, both suspended, as it were, till revealed by the expected close, that very expectation being among the elements of the poet's power.'

Thomson employs the stanza in his 'Castle of Indolence'; Shenstone, in his 'Schoolmistress'; Beattie, in his 'Minstrel'; Burns, in his 'Cotter's Saturday Night'; Campbell, in his 'Gertrude of Wyoming'; Sir Walter Scott, in his 'Don Roderick'; Wordsworth, in his 'Female Vagrant' ('Guilt and Sorrow') and 'Stanzas written in my pocket-copy of Thomson's "Castle of Indolence"'; Shelley, in his 'Revolt of Islam' and his 'Adonais'; Keats, in his 'Eve of St. Agnes'; Croly, in his 'Angel of the World,' and his 'Paris, in 1815'; Lord Byron, in his 'Childe Harold'; Tennyson, in the opening of his 'Lotos-Eaters,' etc.

Space will not allow adequate examples to be given from all these poets; but the student of verse who is interested in noting the varied tones which the same instrument may have under the hands of different performers, due, in part, to the different song which was in each when he wrote, should read (aloud, of course) the first book, at least, of the 'Faerie Queene,' and then the above-mentioned poems.

An indispensable condition of the appreciation of poetic forms is a well-cultivated voice. Without a proper vocal rendering, no poetry, worth reading, can be duly appreciated. The articulating thought may be got through silent reading; but the indefinite, informing spirit can be reached, if reached at all, only through a proper vocal rendition of the verse.

Thomson's 'Castle of Indolence.'

Thomson, in his 'Castle of Indolence,' has, perhaps, most successfully reproduced Spenser's softness and dreaminess of tone. The following stanzas afford good illustrations:

2.

In lowly dale, fast by a river's side,
With woody hill o'er hill encompassed round,
A most enchanting wizard did abide,
Than whom a fiend more fell is nowhere found.
It was, I ween, a lovely spot of ground:
And there a season atween June and May,
Half prankt with spring, with summer half imbrowned,
A listless climate made, where, sooth to say,
No living wight could work, ne caréd even for play.

3.

Was nought around but images of rest :
Sleep-soothing groves, and quiet lawns between ;
And flowery beds that slumbrous influence kest,
From poppies breathed ; and beds of pleasant green,
Where never yet was creeping creature seen.
Meantime, unnumbered glittering streamlets played,
And hurlèd every where their waters sheen ;
That, as they bickered through the sunny glade,
Though restless still themselves, a lulling murmur made.

4.

Joined to the prattle of the purling rills
Were heard the lowing herds along the vale,
And flocks loud bleating from the distant hills,
And vacant shepherds piping in the dale :
And, now and then, sweet Philomel would wail,
Or stock doves plain amid the forest deep,
That drowsy rustled to the sighing gale :
And still a coil the grasshopper did keep :
Yet all these sounds yblent inclinèd all to sleep.

5.

Full, in the passage of the vale, above,
A sable, silent, solemn forest stood,
Where nought but shadowy forms was seen to move,
As Idless fancied in her dreaming mood ;
And up the hills, on either side, a wood
Of blackening pines, aye waving to and fro,
Sent forth a sleepy horror through the blood ;
And where this valley winded out, below,
The murmuring main was heard, and scarcely heard, to flow

6.

A pleasing land of drowsy-head it was,
Of dreams that wave before the half-shut eye ;
And of gay castles in the clouds that pass,
For ever flushing round a summer-sky :
There eke the soft delights, that witchingly

Instil a wanton sweetness through the breast;
And the calm pleasures always hovered nigh;
But whate'er smacked of noyance, or unrest,
Was far, far off expelled from this delicious nest.

Shelley's ' Laon and Cythna.'

In the Preface to ' Laon and Cythna,' better known
as 'The Revolt of Islam,' Shelley says: 'I have
adopted the stanza of Spenser (a measure inex-
pressibly beautiful), not because I consider it a finer
model of poetical harmony than the blank verse of
Shakespeare and Milton, but because in the latter
there is no shelter for mediocrity: you must either
succeed or fail. This perhaps an aspiring spirit should
desire. But I was enticed, also, by *the brilliancy and
magnificence of sound which a mind that has been
nourished upon musical thoughts, can produce by a just
and harmonious arrangement of the pauses of this
measure.'*

'The Revolt of Islam' is more genuinely and
intensely lyrical in its character than is any other
poem in which the stanza is used. The poem is
the expression of a lofty, aspiring, but feverish
and much-bewildered spirit, who, at times, brings
out of the instrument employed all its capabilities of 'brilliancy and magnificence of sound.' But
the reader of 'The Revolt of Islam' cannot but
feel that the instrument was constructed for the
expression of other states and attitudes of mind
and feeling than are generally exhibited in this
poem.

John Todhunter, in 'A Study of Shelley,' remarks:
'In choosing the Spenserian stanza for his great
visionary poem, Shelley challenges comparison with
Spenser himself, and with Byron; and it cannot be
said that he appears to advantage in this comparison.
. . . Compare the impetuous rapidity and pale
intensity of Shelley's verse with the lulling harmony,
the lingering cadence, the voluptuous color of
Spenser's, or with the grandiose majesty of Byron's.
The stanzas of the "Faerie Queene" have something of the wholesome old-world mellowness of
Haydn's music; those of "Laon and Cythna"
something of the morbid fever of Chopin's; . . .
In "Adonais," indeed, a poem on which he bestowed much labor, he handles the stanza in a
masterly manner, and endows it with an individual
music beautiful and new; and even "Laon and
Cythna" is full of exquisite passages, in which the
very rhymes lend wings to his imagination, and
become the occasion of sweet out-of-the-way modes
of expression, full of ethereal poetry of the most
Shelleyan kind.'

The first fifteen stanzas of Canto I afford good
examples of Shelley's use of the stanza in 'The Revolt
of Islam.' The pause-melody constitutes an important
element of the general æsthetic impression; and the
frequent extra end-syllables, resulting in female rhymes,
are skilfully employed, and often with fine musical
effect.

The poet, from 'the peak of an aërial promontory,'
beholds, in the air, 'an Eagle and a Serpent wreathed
in fight ':

When the last hope of trampled France had failed
Like a brief dream of unremaining glory,
From visions of despair I rose, and scaled
The peak of an aërial promontory,
Whose caverned base with the vext surge was hoary;
And saw the golden dawn break forth, and waken
Each cloud, and every wave: — but transitory
The calm: for sudden, the firm earth was shaken,
As if by the last wreck its frame were overtaken.

So as I stood,[1] one blast of muttering thunder
Burst in far peals along the waveless deep,
When, gathering fast, around, above and under,
Long trains of tremulous mist began to creep,
Until their complicating lines did steep
The orient sun in shadow: — not a sound
Was heard; one horrible repose did keep
The forests and the floods, and all around
Darkness more dread than night was poured upon the ground.

Hark ! 'tis the rushing of a wind that sweeps
Earth and the ocean.   See ! the lightnings yawn
Deluging Heaven with fire, and the lashed deeps
Glitter and boil beneath : it rages on,
One mighty stream, whirlwind and waves upthrown.
Lightning, and hail, and darkness eddying by.
There is a pause — the sea-birds, that were gone
Into their caves to shriek, come forth, to spy
What calm has fallen on earth, what light is in the sky.

For, where the irresistible storm had cloven
That fearful darkness, the blue sky was seen
Fretted with many a fair cloud interwoven
Most delicately, and the ocean green,
Beneath that opening spot of blue serene,
Quivered like burning emerald : calm was spread
On all below; but far on high, between
Earth and the upper air, the vast clouds fled,
Countless and swift as leaves on autumn's tempest shed.

---

[1] As I stood thus. — FORMAN.

For ever, as the war became more fierce
Between the whirlwinds and the wrack on high
That spot grew more serene; blue light did pierce
The woof of those white clouds, which seemed to lie
Far, deep, and motionless; while thro' the sky
The pallid semicircle of the moon
Past on, in slow and moving majesty;
Its upper horn arrayed in mists, which soon
But slowly fled, like dew beneath the beams of noon.

I could not choose but gaze; a fascination
Dwelt in that moon, and sky, and clouds, which drew
My fancy thither, and in expectation
Of what I knew not, I remained: — the hue
Of the white moon, amid that heaven so blue,
Suddenly stained with shadow did appear;
A speck, a cloud, a shape, approaching grew,
Like a great ship in the sun's sinking sphere
Beheld afar at sea, and swift it came anear.

Even like a bark, which from a chasm of mountains,
Dark, vast, and overhanging, on a river
Which there collects the strength of all its fountains,
Comes forth, whilst with the speed its frame doth quiver,
Sails, oars, and stream, tending to one endeavour;
So, from that chasm of light a wingèd Form
On all the winds of heaven approaching ever
Floated, dilating as it came: the storm
Pursued it with fierce blasts, and lightnings swift and warm.

A course precipitous, of dizzy speed,
Suspending thought and breath; a monstrous sight!
For in the air do I behold indeed
An Eagle and a Serpent wreathed in fight: —
And now relaxing its impetuous flight,
Before the aërial rock on which I stood,
The Eagle, hovering, wheeled to left and right,
And hung with lingering wings over the flood,
And startled with its yells the wide air's solitude.

A shaft of light upon its wings descended,
And every golden feather gleamed therein —
Feather and scale inextricably blended.[1]
The Serpent's mailed and many-coloured skin
Shone thro' the plumes its coils were twined within
By many a swollen and knotted fold, and high
And far, the neck receding lithe and thin,
Sustained a crested head, which warily
Shifted and glanced before the Eagle's steadfast eye.

Around, around, in ceaseless circles wheeling
With clang of wings and scream, the Eagle sailed
Incessantly — sometimes on high concealing
Its lessening orbs, sometimes as if it failed,
Drooped thro' the air, and still it shrieked and wailed,
And casting back its eager head, with beak
And talon unremittingly assailed
The wreathèd Serpent, who did ever seek
Upon his enemy's heart a mortal wound to wreak.

What life, what power, was kindled and arose
Within the sphere of that appalling fray!
For, from the encounter of those wondrous foes,
A vapour, like the sea's suspended spray
Hung gathered: in the void air, far away,
Floated the shattered plumes; bright scales did leap,
Where'er the Eagle's talons made their way,
Like sparks into the darkness; — as they sweep,
Blood stains the snowy foam of the tumultuous deep.

[1] I suspect the period at the end of this line and the pause at the end of the preceding one should change places. I leave matters as Shelley left them, because there may have been no oversight, the present construction being possible; but it would be more clearly sequent to read the passage thus: ' A shaft of light descended on the eagle's wings, and every golden feather in them gleamed. Feather and scale being blended inextricably, the serpent's mailed and many-coloured skin shone through the plumes,' etc. — FORMAN.

Swift chances in that combat — many a check,
And many a change, a dark and wild turmoil;
Sometimes the Snake around his enemy's neck
Locked in stiff rings his adamantine coil,
Until the Eagle, faint with pain and toil,
Remitted his strong flight, and near the sea
Languidly fluttered, hopeless so to foil
His adversary, who then reared on high
His red and burning crest, radiant with victory.

Then on the white edge of the bursting surge,
Where they had sunk together, would the Snake
Relax his suffocating grasp, and scourge
The wind with his wild writhings; for to break
That chain of torment, the vast bird would shake
The strength of his unconquerable wings
As in despair, and with his sinewy neck,
Dissolve in sudden shock those linkèd rings,
Then soar — as swift as smoke from a volcano springs.

Wile baffled wile, and strength encountered strength,
Thus long, but unprevailing: — the event
Of that portentous fight appeared at length:
Until the lamp of day was almost spent
It had endured, when lifeless,[1] stark, and rent,
Hung high that mighty Serpent, and at last
Fell to the sea, while o'er the continent,
With clang of wings and scream the Eagle past,
Heavily borne away on the exhausted blast.

And with it fled the tempest, so that ocean
And earth and sky shone thro' the atmosphere —
Only, 'twas strange to see the red commotion
Of waves like mountains o'er the sinking sphere
Of sun-set sweep, and their fierce roar to hear
Amid the calm: down the steep path I wound
To the sea-shore - the evening was most clear
And beautiful, and there the sea I found
Calm as a cradled child in dreamless slumber bound.

[1] *Lifeless* is either an oversight or meant to imply *exhausted* merely,
as we learn further on that the snake was still alive. — FORMAN.

English poetry affords no better illustrations of the capabilities of the Spenserian stanza, mentioned by Shelley, in the passage quoted above, than these stanzas afford.

Shelley's ' Adonais.'

After reading the first canto of ' The Revolt of Islam,' which will be sufficient, in order to feel the moulding spirit of the verse, the student should read ' Adonais,' the elegiac tone of which he will feel to be in very decided contrast to the tone of the former poem. ' Adonais,' too, exhibits capabilities of the Spenserian stanza not exhibited, to the same extent, by any other poem written in this stanza.

Every reader, in passing from ' The Revolt of Islam ' (great as are the peculiar merits of its verse) to the ' Adonais,' must feel that the employment of the Spenserian stanza, in the service of the lofty elegiac tone of the latter, is far more successful than its employment as an organ of the tumultuous spirit of the former poem. The following stanzas afford a sufficient evidence of this:

II.

Where wert thou mighty Mother, when he lay,
When thy Son lay, pierced by the shaft which flies
In darkness? Where was lorn Urania
When Adonais died? with veilèd eyes,
'Mid listening Echoes, in her Paradise
She sate, while one, with soft enamoured breath,
Rekindled all the fading melodies,
With which, like flowers that mock the corse beneath,
He had adorned and hid the coming bulk of death.

XIV.

All he had loved, and moulded into thought,
From shape, and hue, and odour, and sweet sound,
Lamented Adonais. Morning sought
Her eastern watchtower, and her hair unbound,
Wet with the tears which should adorn the ground,
Dimmed the aerial eyes that kindle day ;
Afar the melancholy thunder moaned,
Pale Ocean in unquiet slumber lay,
And the wild winds flew around,[1] sobbing in their dismay.

The alexandrine of this stanza has a special effectiveness by reason of its two exceptional feet, the third foot 'flew around,' being an *xxa*, and the fourth, 'sobbing,' an *ax*. In reading the verse, the voice should be well filled out on 'wild winds,' accelerated on 'flew a-,' and brought down strongly on 'round '; the exceptional ictus on 'sob-' is effective. Peter Bayne quotes this stanza in his 'Tennyson and his Teachers,' and remarks of it : 'If absolute perfection could be asserted of any human thing, that stanza might be called perfect ; utterly faultless, at once in feeling, imagery, diction, and rhythm.'

XVIII.

Ah, woe is me! Winter is come and gone,
But grief returns with the revolving year ;
The airs and streams renew their joyous tone ;
The ants, the bees, the swallows, re-appear :
Fresh leaves and flowers deck the dead Seasons' bier ;
The amorous birds now pair in every brake,
And build their mossy homes in field and brere ;
And the green lizard, and the golden snake,
Like unimprisoned flames, out of their trance awake.

---

[1] 'Around,' according to Mrs. Shelley's editions ; Forman's edition has 'round,' which is less effective.

XIX.

Through wood and stream and field and hill and Ocean
A quickening life from the Earth's heart has burst,
As it has ever done, with change and motion,
From the great morning of the world when first
God dawned on Chaos; in its stream immersed,
The lamps of Heaven flash with a softer light:
All baser things pant with life's sacred thirst,
Diffuse themselves, and spend in love's delight
The beauty and the joy of their renewed might.

XXXI.

Midst others of less note, came one frail Form,[1]
A phantom among men; companionless
As the last cloud of an expiring storm
Whose thunder is its knell: he, as I guess,
Had gazed on Nature's naked loveliness,
Actæon-like, and now he fled astray
With feeble steps o'er the world's wilderness,
And his own thoughts along that rugged way,
Pursued, like raging hounds, their father and their prey.

XXXIII.

His head was bound with pansies overblown,
And faded violets, white, and pied, and blue;
And a light spear topped with a cypress cone,
Round whose rude shaft dark ivy tresses grew
Yet dripping with the forest's noonday dew,
Vibrated,[2] as the ever-beating heart
. Shook the weak hand that grasped it; of that crew
He came the last, neglected and apart:
A herd-abandoned deer, struck by the hunter's dart

---

[1] Shelley here alludes to himself.

[2] Note the effect here of the exceptional ictus, and of the pause after this initial word.

LIV.

That Light whose smile kindles the Universe,
That Beauty in which all things work and move,
That Benediction which the eclipsing Curse
Of birth can quench not, that sustaining Love
Which through the web of being blindly wove
By man and beast and earth and air and sea,
Burns bright or dim, as each are mirrors of
The fire for which all thirst; now beams on me,
Consuming the last clouds of cold mortality.

LV.

The breath whose might I have invoked in song
Descends on me; my spirit's bark is driven,
Far from the shore, far from the trembling throng
Whose sails were never to the tempest given;
The massy earth and sphered skies are riven!
I am borne darkly, fearfully, afar;
Whilst burning through the inmost veil of Heaven,
The soul of Adonais, like a star,
Beacons from the abode where the Eternal are.

Keats's ' Eve of St. Agnes.'

In what Peter Bayne calls 'her lingering, loving,
particularizing mood,' Imagination finds ample scope
in the roomy and elaborately wrought Spenserian
stanza; and the adaptability of the stanza to this
mood, is in no other poem better illustrated than
it is in Keats's ' Eve of St. Agnes.'

'Keats takes in this poem,' says Sidney Colvin,
'the simple, almost threadbare theme of the love
of an adventurous youth for the daughter of a hos-
tile house . . . and brings it deftly into association

with the old popular belief as to the way a maiden might on this anniversary win sight of her lover in a dream. Choosing happily for such a purpose the Spenserian stanza, he adds to the melodious grace, the "sweet-slipping movement," as it has been called, of Spenser, a transparent ease and directness of construction; and with this ease and directness combines . . . a never-failing richness and concentration of poetic meaning and suggestion.'

Of these high merits the following stanzas afford signal illustrations :

I.

St. Agnes' Eve — Ah, bitter chill it was!
The owl, for all his feathers, was a-cold ;
The hare limped trembling through the frozen grass,
And silent was the flock in wooly fold ;
Numb were the beadsman's fingers while he told
His rosary, and while his frosted breath,
Like pious incense from a censer old,
Seemed taking flight for heaven without a death
Past the sweet Virgin's picture, while his prayer he saith.

II.

His prayer he saith, this patient, holy man,
Then takes his lamp, and riseth from his knees,
And back returneth, meagre, barefoot, wan,
Along the chapel aisle by slow degrees :
The sculptured dead on each side seem to freeze,
Emprisoned in black, purgatorial rails :
Knights, ladies, praying in dumb orat'ries,
He passeth by ; and his weak spirit fails
To think how they may ache in icy hoods and mails.[1]

---

[1] The monuments in the chapel aisle are brought before us, not by any effort of description, but solely through our sympathy with the shivering fancy of the beadsman. — SIDNEY COLVIN.

The ancient Beadsman heard the prelude soft ;
And so it chanced, for many a door was wide,
From hurry to and fro. Soon, up aloft,
The silver, snarling trumpets 'gan to chide :
The level chambers, ready with their pride,
Were glowing to receive a thousand guests :
The carvèd angels, ever eager-eyed,
Stared, where upon their heads the cornice rests,
With hair blown back, and wings put cross-wise on their breasts.[1]

A fine effect is secured by the pause after the
initial word ' Stared,' of the eighth verse. The word
should be read with a downward inflection. The
emphasis upon it is increased by its receiving an
irregular ictus. The alexandrine is one of the best,
and most picturesque, in the poem.

XXIV.

A casement high and triple-arched there was,
All garlanded with carven imageries
Of fruits, and flowers, and bunches of knot-grass,
And diamonded with panes of quaint device,
Innumerable of stains and splendid dyes,
As are the tiger-moth's deep-damasked wings ;[2]
And in the midst, 'mong thousand heraldries,
And twilight saints, and dim emblazonings,
A shielded scutcheon blushed with blood of queens and kings.[3]

[1] Even into the sculptured heads of the corbels in the banqueting-hall the poet strikes life. — SIDNEY COLVIN.

[2] A gorgeous phrase which leaves the widest range to the colour-imagination of the reader, giving it at the same time a sufficient clue by the simile drawn from a particular specimen of nature's blazonry. — SIDNEY COLVIN.

[3] The word ' blush ' makes the colour seem to come and go, while the mind is at the same time sent travelling from the maiden's chamber on thoughts of her lineage and ancestral fame. — SIDNEY COLVIN.

XXV.

Full on this casement shone the wintry moon,
And threw warm gules on Madeline's fair breast,
As down she knelt for heaven's grace and boon ;
Rose-bloom fell on her hands together prest,
And on her silver cross soft amethyst,
And on her hair a glory like a saint : [1]
She seemed a splendid angel, newly drest,
Save wings, for heaven : — Porphyro grew faint,
She knelt, so pure a thing, so free from mortal taint.

XXVI.

Anon his heart revives : her vespers done.
Of all its wreathed pearls her hair she frees :
Unclasps her warmèd jewels one by one ; [2]
Loosens her fragrant bodice ; by degrees
Her rich attire creeps rustling to her knees :
Half-hidden, like a mermaid in sea-weed,
Pensive a while she dreams awake, and sees,
In fancy, fair St. Agnes in her bed,
But dares not look behind, or all the charm is fled.

XXVII.

Soon, trembling in her soft and chilly nest
In sort of wakeful swoon, perplexed she lay,
Until the poppied warmth of sleep oppressed
Her soothed limbs, and soul fatigued away
Flown, like a thought, until the morrow day ;

---

[1] Observation, I believe, shows that moonlight has not the power to transmit the hues of the painted glass as Keats in this celebrated passage represents it. Let us be grateful for the error, if error it is, which has led him to heighten by these saintly splendors of colour, the sentiment of a scene wherein a voluptuous glow is so exquisitely attempered with chivalrous chastity and awe. — SIDNEY COLVIN.

[2] When Madeline unclasps her jewels, a weaker poet would have dwelt on their lustre or other visible qualities; Keats puts those aside, and speaks straight to our spirits in an epithet breathing with the very life of the wearer — 'her warmèd jewels.' — SIDNEY COLVIN.

Blissfully havened both from joy and pain ;
Clasped like a missal where swart Paynims pray ;
Blinded alike from sunshine and from rain,
As though a rose should shut, and be a bud again.

xxx.

And still she slept an azure-lidded sleep,
In blanched linen, smooth and lavendered,
While he from forth the closet brought a heap
Of candied apple, quince, and plum, and gourd,
With jellies soother than the creamy curd,
And lucent syrups tinct with cinnamon,
Manna and dates, in argosy transferred
From Fez ; and spicèd dainties every one,
From silken Samarcand to cedared Lebanon.[1]

Probably no English poet who has used the Spenserian stanza, first assimilated so fully the spirit of Spenser, before using the stanza, as did Keats ; and to this fact may be partly attributed his effective use of it as an organ for his imagination in its ' lingering, loving, particularizing mood.' His early friend, Charles Cowden Clarke, who introduced him to Spenser, describes his rapturous enjoyment of the ' Faerie Queene.' And another of his friends, Charles Armitage Brown, states that the earliest awakening of his poetical genius was due to Spenser. ' In Spenser's fairyland he was enchanted, breathed in a new world, . . . enamoured of the stanza, he attempted to imitate it,

---

[1] When Lorenzo spreads the feast of dainties beside his sleeping mistress, we are made to feel how those ideal and rare sweets of sense surround and minister to her, not only with their own natural richness, but with the associations and the homage of all far countries whence they have been gathered —

' From silken Samarcand to cedared Lebanon.'
— SIDNEY COLVIN.

and succeeded. . . . This, his earliest attempt, the "Imitation of Spenser," is in his first volume of poems, and it is peculiarly interesting to those acquainted with his history.'

Byron's ' Childe Harold.'

But no English poet has used the Spenserian stanza with the grand *vigor* with which Byron has used it in his 'Childe Harold.' His impetuous spirit imparts a character to the stanza quite distinct from its peculiar Spenserian character. Even the stanzas in which his gentler and more pensive moods are embodied, bear little or no similarity to the manner of Spenser.

The two following stanzas, which were inspired by the battlefield of Albuera, are good examples of the Byronic vigor:

> Hark ! heard you not those hoofs of dreadful note ?
> Sounds not the clang of conflict on the heath ?
> Saw ye not whom the reeking sabre smote,
> Nor saved your brethren ere they sank beneath
> Tyrants and tyrants' slaves ? — the fires of death,
> The bale-fires flash on high : — from rock to rock
> Each volley tells that thousands cease to breathe ;
> Death rides upon the sulphury Siroc,
> Red Battle stamps his foot, and nations feel the shock.

Note, in this stanza, the unobtrusive but suggestive effect of the alliteration which occurs in each and every verse : 'hark,' 'heard,' 'hoofs'; 'clang of conflict'; 'saw,' 'sabre,' 'smote'; 'saved,' 'brethren,' 'sank,' 'beneath'; 'tyrants and tyrants' slaves'; 'bale-fires flash,' 'rock to rock'; 'tells that thousands cease to breathe'; 'the sulphury Siroc'; 'stamps his foot,' 'feel the shock.' These alliterations are all

taken up into the general effect, and leave no sense
of trick or artifice.   And there are some effective
ones in the stanza which follows: ' Restless it rolls,
now fixed, and now anon flashing afar '; ' destruction,'
' deeds are done '; ' morn,' ' meet '; ' to shed before
his shrine.'

> Lo ! where the giant on the mountain stands,
>   His blood-red tresses deepening in the sun,
> With death-shot glowing in his fiery hands,
>   And eye that scorcheth all it glares upon.
> Restless it rolls, now fixed, and now anon
>   Flashing afar — and at his iron feet
> Destruction cowers to mark what deeds are done :
>   For on this morn three potent nations meet,   .
>   To shed before his shrine the blood he deems most sweet.
>
> — Canto i. st. 38, 39.

And the following, descriptive of a Spanish bull-
fight (alliteration is also in these an important element
of effect ; and so too are the exceptional ictus on the
initial words of some of the verses : ' Bounds with one
lashing spring the mighty brute '; ' Sudden he stops ';
' Streams from his flank '; ' Vain are his weapons ';
' Staggering, but stemming all '; ' Wraps his fierce
eye '; ' Sheathed in his form '; ' Slowly he falls ';
' Hurl the dark bulk ') :

> Thrice sounds the clarion ; lo! the signal falls,
> The den expands, and Expectation mute
> Gapes round the silent circle's peopled walls.
> Bounds with one lashing spring the mighty brute,
> And, wildly staring, spurns, with sounding foot,
> The sand, nor blindly rushes on his foe :
> Here, there, he points his threatening front, to suit
> His first attack, wide waving to and fro
> His angry tail ; red rolls his eye's dilated glow.

Sudden he stops; his eye is fixed: away,
Away, thou heedless boy! prepare the spear:
Now is thy time to perish, or display
The skill that yet may check his mad career.
With well-timed croupe the nimble coursers veer;
On foams the bull, but not unscathed he goes;
Streams from his flank the crimson torrent clear:
He flies, he wheels, distracted with his throes;
Dart follows dart; lance, lance; loud bellowings speak his woes.

Again he comes; nor dart nor lance avail,
Nor the wild plunging of the tortured horse:
Though man and man's avenging arms assail,
Vain are his weapons, vainer is his force.
One gallant steed is stretched a mangled corse;
Another, hideous sight! unseamed appears,
His gory chest unveils life's panting source:
Though death-struck, still his feeble frame he rears;
Staggering, but stemming all, his lord unharmed he bears.

Foiled, bleeding, breathless, furious to the last,
Full in the centre stands the bull at bay,
Mid wounds and clinging darts, and lances brast,
And foes disabled in the brutal fray:
And now the Matadores around him play,
Shake the red cloak and poise the ready brand:
Once more through all he bursts his thundering way —
Vain rage! the mantle quits the conynge hand,
Wraps his fierce eye — 'tis past — he sinks upon the sand!

Where his vast neck just mingles with the spine,
Sheathed in his form the deadly weapon lies.
He stops — he starts — disdaining to decline:
Slowly he falls, amidst triumphant cries,
Without a groan, without a struggle dies.
The decorated car appears — on high
The corse is piled — sweet sight for vulgar eyes —
Four steeds that spurn the rein, as swift as shy,
Hurl the dark bulk along, scarce seen in dashing by.

—Canto i. st. lxxv.-lxxix.

Some of Byron's finest stanzas were inspired by the sea. The following has the sweep of the surge in it:

Once more upon the waters! yet once more!
And the waves bound beneath me as a steed
That knows his rider. Welcome, to the roar!
Swift be their guidance, wheresoe'er it lead!
Though the strained mast should quiver as a reed,
And the rent canvas fluttering strew the gale,
Still must I on; for I am as a weed,
Flung from the rock, on Ocean's foam, to sail
Where'er the surge may sweep, the tempest's breath prevail.
                                        —Canto iii. st. ii.

The stanzas descriptive of the ball at Brussels, and of the battle of Waterloo, are among the most spirited in 'Childe Harold':

There was a sound of revelry by night,
And Belgium's capital had gathered then
Her Beauty and her Chivalry, and bright
The lamps shone o'er fair women and brave men;
A thousand hearts beat happily; and when
Music arose with its voluptuous swell,
Soft eyes looked love to eyes which spoke again,
And all went merry as a marriage-bell;
But hush' hark! a deep sound strikes like a rising knell!

Did ye not hear it?— No; 'twas but the wind
Or the car rattling o'er the stony street;
On with the dance! let joy be unconfined;
No sleep till morn, when Youth and Pleasure meet
To chase the glowing Hours with flying feet —
But, hark! — that heavy sound breaks in once more,
As if the clouds its echo would repeat;
And nearer, clearer, deadlier than before!
Arm! Arm! it is — it is — the cannon's opening roar!

Within a windowed niche of that high hall
Sate Brunswick's fated chieftain ; he did hear
That sound the first amidst the festival,
And caught its tone with Death's prophetic ear ;
And when they smiled because he deemed it near,
His heart more truly knew that peal too well
Which stretched his father on a bloody bier,
And roused the vengeance blood alone could quell :
He rushed into the field, and, foremost fighting, fell.

The alliteration in the alexandrine of this stanza is effective.

And there was mounting in hot haste : the steed,
The mustering squadron, and the clattering car,
Went pouring forward with impetuous speed,
And swiftly forming in the ranks of war ;
And the deep thunder peal on peal afar ;
And near, the beat of the alarming drum
Roused up the soldier ere the morning star ;
While thronged the citizens with terror dumb,
Or whispering, with white lips — ' The foe! They come! they
        come!'
                                    — Canto iii. st. xxi.–xxiii. xxv.

But even finer than these are the stanzas descriptive of a thunderstorm in the Alps. They could only have been written out of a most inspiring sympathy with the storm. The chords of the instrument are struck with an unerring vigor :

The sky is changed! and such a change! O night,
And storm, and darkness, ye are wondrous strong,
Yet lovely in your strength, as is the light
Of a dark eye in woman! Far along,
From peak to peak, the rattling crags among,

Leaps the live thunder! Not from one lone cloud,
But every mountain now hath found a tongue,
And Jura answers, through her misty shroud,
Back to the joyous Alps, who call to her aloud!

And this is in the night: — most glorious night!
Thou wert not sent for slumber! let me be
A sharer in thy fierce and far delight, —
A portion of the tempest and of thee![1]
How the lit lake shines, a phosphoric sea,
And the big rain comes dancing to the earth!
And now again 'tis black, — and now, the glee
Of the loud hills shakes with its mountain-mirth,
As if they did rejoice o'er a young earthquake's birth.

— Canto iii. st. xcii. xciii.

In contrast with the impetuous spirit embodied in
all the preceding stanzas, is the gentle mood which
informs the following stanza, descriptive of a quiet
night-scene on Lake Leman:

It is the hush of night, and all between
Thy margin and the mountains, dark, yet clear,
Mellowed and mingling, yet distinctly seen,
Save darkened Jura, whose capt heights appear
Precipitously steep; and drawing near,
There breathes a living fragrance from the shore,
Of flowers yet fresh with childhood; on the ear
Drops the light drip of the suspended oar,
Or chirps the grasshopper one good-night carol more.

— Canto iii. st. lxxxvi.

Perhaps the most delicious stanzas in 'Childe
Harold' are those descriptive of the fountain of
Egeria:

[1] The thunder-storm to which these lines refer occurred on the 13th
of June, 1816, at midnight. I have seen, among the Acroceraunian
mountains of Chimari, several more terrible, but none more beautiful.
— BYRON's *Note*.

Egeria ! sweet creation of some heart
Which found no mortal resting-place so fair
As thine ideal breast ; whate'er thou art
Or wert, — a young Aurora of the air,
The nympholepsy of some fond despair :
Or, it might be, a beauty of the earth,
Who found a more than common votary there
Too much adoring ; whatsoe'er thy birth,
Thou wert a beautiful thought, and softly bodied forth.

The mosses of thy fountain still are sprinkled
With thine Elysian water-drops ; the face
Of thy cave-guarded spring, with years unwrinkled,
Reflects the meek-eyed genius of the place,
Whose green, wild margin now no more erase
Art's works ; nor must the delicate waters sleep,
Prisoned in marble ; bubbling from the base
Of the cleft statue, with a gentle leap
The rill runs o'er, and round, fern, flowers, and ivy. creep,

Fantastically tangled :

Here the alexandrine is not sufficient to fill out the
measure of the poet's musing on the creeping ferns
and ivies, and so it runs uninterruptedly on into the
middle of the first verse of the next stanza :

The rill runs o'er, and round, fern, flowers, and ivy creep,

Fantastically tangled ; the green hills
Are clothed with early blossoms, through the grass
The quick-eyed lizard rustles, and the bills
Of summer-birds sing welcome as ye pass ;
Flowers fresh in hue, and many in their class,
Implore the pausing step, and with their dyes
Dance in the soft breeze in a fairy mass :
The sweetness of the violet's deep-blue eyes,
Kissed by the breath of heaven, seems coloured by its skies.

—Canto iv. st. cxv.–cxvii

Tennyson's ' Lotos-Eaters.'

The first five stanzas of Tennyson's 'Lotos-Eaters'
are Spenserian, and they are quite unique in character. One familiar with the ' Faerie Queene ' and with
all other poems in the literature in which the stanza
is used, might read these five stanzas many times
without thinking of their being Spenserian in construction. All the prolongable vowels of the language
predominate; and many of these are encased in a
framework of prolongable consonants. A long-drawn
time, and a peculiar toning are thus imparted to the
verse, which subserve most effectively the theme of
the poem. The following is the third stanza :

> The charmèd sunset lingered low adown
> In the red West : through mountain clefts the dale
> Was seen far inland, and the yellow down
> Bordered with palm, and many a winding vale
> And meadow, set with slender galingale :
> A land where all things always seemed the same!
> And round about the keel with faces pale,
> Dark faces pale against that rosy flame,
> The mild-eyed melancholy Lotos-eaters came.

The many examples which have been given of the
Spenserian stanza, from Spenser, Thomson, Shelley,
Keats, Byron, and Tennyson, bear testimony to its
almost unlimited capabilities. But a comparatively
small part of those capabilities have been illustrated.
There is certainly no other group of rhyming verses
in the literature, which surpasses it in capabilities.
This stanza, the dramatic blank verse of Shakespeare,
in its most advanced development, and the epic blank

verse of Milton, with its unlimited capacity of varied grouping, are the noblest poetic forms which have been developed in English literature.

. After reading the several poems enumerated, written in the Spenserian stanza, the student may not be able to formulate very distinctly his impressions of the differences in tone, color, and moulding-spirit which they exhibit; but it is not necessary that he should do so. The important thing is that he have a decided consciousness of these differences; he may then rest content with a very general formulation of them, or with no formulation at all. The tendency toward a precipitation of what is held in solution, in a poetical composition, and a crystallization of it into the abstract, needs no special encouragement in these days. One aim of literary culture should be, to make the concrete, as far as possible, a direct language; rather than to regard it as a foreign language to be translated into the more familiar language of the intellect. The spiritual nature can be vitalized only through the concrete, and the personal — through a sympathetic assimilation of these. Without a susceptibility to form, no one can come into the most intimate relationship with a product of poetic genius. He may know its articulating thought; but its essential life is something other than that.

THE INFLUENCE OF THE SPENSERIAN STANZA ON OTHER MODES OF STANZA-STRUCTURE.

SPENSER'S effective use of the alexandrine caused this verse to be used by many succeeding poets as a final verse to their stanzas, for the purpose of securing a strong terminal emphasis, and of imparting a long-drawn-out close.

Two professed imitators of Spenser employ it, Phineas Fletcher, in his 'Purple Island' (1633, but written some years earlier), and Giles Fletcher, called 'the Spenser of his age,' in his 'Christ's Victory and Triumph' (1640).

The stanza of the 'Purple Island' is composed of seven verses, six being 5 xa, and the seventh an alexandrine. The rhyme-scheme is *ababccc*. The last three verses rhyming together, the resulting rhyme-emphasis mars the emphasis-symmetry of the stanza, especially when the rhymes are double rhymes, as they frequently are. For example (the poet is describing the happiness of the shepherd's life) :

His bed of wool yields safe and quiet sleeps,
While by his side his faithful spouse hath place ;
His little son into his bosom creeps,
The lively picture of his father's face :
Never his humble house nor state torment him :
Less he could like, if less his God had sent him ;
And when he dies, green turfs, with grassy tomb, content him.

134

The terminal rhyme-emphasis here is too pronounced, and makes the stanza lop-sided ; the rhymes have a thumping effect which is almost ludicrous.

The stanza of 'Christ's Victory and Triumph' is composed of eight verses, seven being 5 *xa*, and the eighth, an alexandrine. The rhyme-scheme is *ababbccc*. The emphasis-symmetry of the stanza is somewhat better than that of the 'Purple Island,' by reason of the fifth verse receiving a second rhyme, which serves to graduate somewhat the rhyme-emphasis of the stanza.

The following stanza is a little above the average in merit :

> Witness the thunder that mount Sinai heard,
> When all the hill with fiery clouds did flame,
> And wandering Israel, with the sight afeard,
> Blinded with seeing, durst not touch the same,
> But like a wood of shaking leaves became.
> On this dead Justice, she, the Living Law,
> Bowing herself with a majestic awe,
> All heaven, to hear her speech, did into silence draw.

Sometimes the rhyme in the last three verses is on the same vowel as that of one of the rhymes of the first five, and the assonance is felt to be excessive ; and worse, still, the rhyme (evidently by chance) in the last three verses is sometimes a continuation of one of the first five. The following stanza affords an example of this, in which there is also a repetition of a final word (wore) :

> About her head a cypress heaven she wore,
> Spread like a veil, upheld with silver wire,
> In which the stars so burnt in golden ore,
> As seemed the azure web was all on fire :

> But hastily, to quench their sparkling ire,
> A flood of milk came rolling up the shore,
> That on his curded wave swift Argus wore,
> And the immortal swan, that did her life deplore.

There is too much of a good thing here in the way of rhyme.

Double rhymes also occur in the last three verses of stanzas, in 'Christ's Victory and Triumph,' which have the thumping effect illustrated by the stanza given from the other poem.

The rhyme-schemes of both poems are quite arbitrary. There is no justification of the accumulated rhyme-emphasis at the end of the stanzas.

Milton, who was a lover of Spenser, and, as is evident, caught from him many metrical effects and graces, has some beautiful alexandrines in his ode 'On the Morning of Christ's Nativity.'

In the stanza employed, fine effects are secured through the varied metres and the disposition of the rhymes.

The verse is regularly *xa*.

The first, second, fourth, and fifth verses are trimeter (3 *xa*).

The third and sixth are pentameter (5 *xa*).

The seventh is tetrameter (4 *xa*).

The eighth is hexameter or alexandrine (6 *xa*).

Each metre in the stanza derives some effect from the other metres, the theme-metre being 3 *xa*.

The rhyme-scheme is *aabccbdd*.

The structure of the stanza, and the beauty and effectiveness of the closing alexandrine are well illustrated by the following stanzas :

V.

But peaceful was the night,
Wherein the Prince of light
 His reign of peace upon the earth began:
The winds with wonder whist,
Smoothly the waters kist,
 Whispering new joys to the mild oceän,
Who now hath quite forgot to rave,
While birds of calm sit brooding on the charmèd wave.

IX.

When such music sweet
Their hearts and ears did greet,
 As never was by mortal finger strook;
Divinely warbled voice
Answering the stringèd noise,
 As all their souls in blissful rapture took:
The air, such pleasure loth to lose,
With thousand echoes still prolongs each heavenly close.

XVI.

But wisest Fate says No
This must not yet be so;
 The Babe yet lies in smiling infancy   •
That on the bitter cross
Must redeem our loss,
 So both himself and us to glorify:
Yet first, to those ychained in sleep,
The wakeful trump of doom must thunder through the deep.[1]

XX.

The lonely mountains o'er,
And the resounding shore,
 A voice of weeping heard and loud lament;
From haunted spring, and dale
Edgèd with poplar pale,
 The parting Genius is with sighing sent;
With flower-inwoven tresses torn,
The nymphs in twilight shade of tangled thickets mourn.

---

[1] This reminds of the fine verse in 'Paradise Lost,' i. 177: 'To
bellow through the vast and boundless deep.'

The stanza of Milton's elegy 'On the death of a fair infant,' and of 'The Passion,' distinctly reflects the Spenserian stanza. It is composed of six 5-*ra* verses and an alexandrine, the rhyme-scheme being *ababbcc*.

The following is the fifth stanza of the elegy:

> Yet can I not persuade me thou art dead,
> Or that thy corse corrupts in earth's dark womb,
> Or that thy beauties lie in wormy bed
> Hid from the world in a low-delvèd tomb;
> Could Heaven for pity thee so strictly [1] doom ?
> Oh no! for something in thy face did shine
> Above mortality, that showed thou wast divine.

This is a much superior stanza to the stanza of Phineas Fletcher's 'Purple Island,' and of Giles Fletcher's 'Christ's Victory and Triumph,' the rhyme-schemes of which are *ababcc* and *ababbccc*, respectively.

One of Pope's alexandrines, a quite Spenserian one, should be noticed here. It occurs in his translation of the 'Odyssey,' in the description of the labor of Sisyphus (Bk. xi. 735-738); and note the monosyllabic second verse, with its suggestive aspirates. The exceptional ictus on the initial word 'Thunders' of the alexandrine, is also effective:

> With many a weary step and many a groan,
> Up the high hill he heaves a huge round stone:
> The huge round stone, resulting with a bound,
> Thunders impetuous down, and smokes along the ground.

---

[1] Strictly: *straitly, narrowly,* referring to 'low delvèd tomb.'

This is certainly not what Pope, in his 'Essay on Criticism' (*v.* 356), calls 'a needless alexandrine,'

That, like a wounded snake, drags its slow length along.

One other offspring of the Spenserian stanza must be noticed — an unworthy one — namely, that of Matthew Prior's 'Ode on the battle of Ramillies' (1706). It is composed of two quatrains, with independent alternate rhyme-schemes, and a couplet of a pentameter and an alexandrine, the rhyme-scheme being *ababcdcdee*. By adding a verse to the Spenserian stanza, Prior thought that he 'made the number more *harmonious*.' Guest remarks ('History of English Rhythms,' Vol. 2, p. 394): 'Had he stated *facility* to be his aim, he had shown more honesty. He has escaped the difficulties of Spenser's stanza, but at the same time has sacrificed all its *science* and not a little of its beauty.'

Doctor Johnson speaks of Prior's stanza as 'an uniform mass of ten lines thirty-five times repeated. . . . He has altered the stanza of Spenser, as a house is altered by building another in its place of a different form.'

It will be found worth while to read some of these thirty-five stanzas, along with some of Spenser's, in order to feel very distinctly the difference between an organic structure of verse and a mechanical one.

One of the most notable lyrical stanzas in English poetry, in which a final alexandrine is employed in the service of the lyrical gush, is that of Shelley's 'Ode to a Skylark.'

The stanza of this beautiful ode is composed of five verses. The rhythm of the first four is *ax*, and the metre is trimeter, the third and fourth verses being catalectic or defective (that is, the last foot lacks the light syllable). The fifth verse is an alexandrine (6 *xa*), the rhythm being the reverse of that of the other verses. This verse also receives a second rhyme, rhyming with the second and fourth verses of the stanza, — the rhyme-scheme being *ababb*. Here, then, are nearly all the means of enforcement employed upon the concluding verse: 1. It is double the length of the other verses (more than double that of the second and fourth); 2. Its rhythm is the reverse of that of the other verses; 3. A second rhyme falls upon it; 4. The poet has, in most cases, imparted to it an extra vowel and consonant melody. The effect of the ode, when read aloud, is that of a succession of strong gushes of feeling.

To revert to what has been said in regard to the unifying action of feeling: the stronger, more impetuous, more lyrical the emotion of the poet, the more compact will be the resultant unities; the rhythm, which is a succession of the primal unities, will be more marked; verses will be more strongly individualized by means of melody and rhyme, and other means to which attention has been called; and stanzas will be more closely bound together by means of harmony, rhyme, etc.

As poetical emotion descends and thought ascends, these unities, where the form is organic, not mechanical, become looser, so to speak, until, as in Shakespeare's more mature dramatic blank verse, their outlines are quite lost, and the language is little more than faintly throbbing prose.

I.

Hail to thee, blithe spirit!
  Bird thou never wert,
That from heaven or near it,
  Pourest thy full heart,
In profuse strains of unpremeditated art.

II.

Higher still and higher
  From the earth thou springest,
Like a cloud of fire
  The blue deep thou wingest,
And singing, still dost soar, and soaring, ever singest.

XII.

Sound of vernal showers
  On the twinkling grass,
Rain-awakened flowers,
  All that ever was
Joyous, and clear, and fresh, thy music doth surpass.

XXI.

Teach me half the gladness
  That thy brain must know;
Such harmonious madness
  Through my lips would flow,
The world should listen then as I am listening now.

The analyses which have been presented of some of the more important stanzas of English poetry, will enable the student, it is hoped, to analyze other stanzas, and to show their peculiar capabilities.

The organic character of a stanza must, of course, first be *felt*. A cold-blooded analysis avails nothing.

The true object of an analysis is to discover some of the secrets of an effect previously experienced.

But a stanza may have been arbitrarily adopted. Even then, its want of adaptedness to the theme must first be felt ; and it will be the object of analysis to show that it is a ready-made, ill-fitting vesture, rather than an organic form moulded by feeling.

X.

THE SONNET.

ENGLISH Poetry is indebted to the Italian for
one of its most important art-forms, which, under
various modifications, has been employed by several
of the greatest of English poets for the embodiment
of some of their subtlest feelings, and noblest and
most spiritualized thoughts. In his sonnet on the
'Sonnet,' Wordsworth, the greatest of English Son-
neteers, says :

> with this key
> Shakespeare unlocked his heart ; . . .
> a glowworm lamp,
> It cheered mild Spenser, called from Faery Land
> To struggle with dark ways ; and when a damp
> Fell round the path of Milton, in his hand
> The thing became a trumpet, whence he blew
> Soul-animating strains — alas, too few'!

And in another of his sonnets, he says :

> to me,
> In sundry moods, 'twas pastime to be bound
> Within the Sonnet's scanty plot of ground :
> Pleased if some Souls (for such there needs must be)
> Who have felt the weight of too much liberty,
> Should find brief solace there, as I have found.

After setting forth the strict rules to which the
sonnet is subject, Archbishop Trench asks : 'What

are the advantages which the sonnet offers to com-
pensate for the difficulties which it presents, for the
restraints which it imposes? Why has the sonnet
been, with poets at least, I speak not now of their
readers, so favourite a metre? They have, in the
first place, felt, no doubt, the advantage of that check
to diffuseness, that necessity of condensation and concentration which these narrow limits impose. Often-
times a poem which, except for these, would have
been but a loose nebulous vapour, has been com-
pressed and rounded into a star. . . . The sonnet,
like a Grecian temple, may be limited in its scope,
but like that, if successful, it is altogether perfect.'

The greatest of the Italian sonnet writers are
Petrarch, Dante, Tasso, Ariosto, Michel Angelo, and
Vittoria Colonna; and to these masters we must
look for the best types of this poetical structure.
And it will be found that those sonnets, in English
poetry, which conform most closely to these types,
in form and function, are, in general, the most satisfying, though it will be seen that many of the noblest
English sonnets violate, in some respects, the Italian
sonnet legislation, while securing the peculiar art-
effect of the sonnet.

That peculiar art-effect, in its best and deepest
form, is well, though somewhat loftily, expressed in
the sestet of a sonnet by Theodore Watts, entitled
'The Sonnet's Voice. A metrical lesson by the sea-
shore':

> Yon silvery billows breaking on the beach
>   Fall back in foam beneath the star-shine clear,
>   The while my rhymes are murmuring in your ear
> A restless lore like that the billows teach;

For on these sonnet-waves my soul would reach
    From its own depths, and rest within you, dear,
    As, through the billowy voices yearning here
Great Nature strives to find a human speech.

A sonnet is a wave of melody :
    From heaving waters of the impassioned soul
    A billow of tidal music one and whole
Flows in the ' octave '; then, returning free,
    Its ebbing surges in the ' sestet ' roll
Back to the deeps of Life's tumultuous sea.[1]

The perfection to which the sonnet has been brought, in the land of its birth, and its extensive use by all grades of poetical ability, testify to the intrinsic value of it as a poetical organ, and the high estimation in which it has for centuries been held. And this high estimation, while it has resulted in many 'a thing of beauty' which will be 'a joy forever,' has also resulted in the production of thousands of worthless specimens, by poetasters who made of it a literary plaything.

In the production of a sonnet of triumphant success, heart, head, and hand must be right. If they are not, there is no other poetical form which is such a tell-tale, and which so reveals all the shortcomings and disqualifications of its author. 'Apart from all sanctions, the student of poetry knows that no form of verse is a surer touchstone of mastery than this, which is so easy to write badly, so supremely difficult to write well, so full both of hindrance and of occasion

---

[1] First published in the London *Athenæum*, September 17th, 1881, and quoted in preface (p. xxi) of ' Sonnets of Three Centuries.' Edited by T. Hall Caine, London, 1882.

in all matters of structure and style; neither any a
more searching test of inspiration, since on the one
hand it seems to provoke the affectations of ingenuity,
and on the other hand it has been chosen by the
greatest men of all as the medium for their most
intimate, direct, and overwhelming self-disclosures.'[1]
'The steadiness of hand and clearness of mind required for rounding into the invariable limit of fourteen
iambic lines some weighty matter of thought or
delicate subtlety of feeling is not easy to overrate.'[2]

The first requirement of a sonnet is that it consist
of fourteen 5.*ra* verses. The second is, that these
fourteen verses be *organically* divided into an octave
and a sestet (the former subdivided into two quatrains,
the latter into two tercets); which organic divisions
must have distinct rhyme-schemes, as exponents of
their separate functions. Furthermore, the rhymes
in the sestet must not clash in any way with those in
the octave. Their vowels should be different, and so
should their consonant framework, otherwise the distinctness of the two rhyme-schemes is somewhat
reduced.

But there are hundreds of English sonnets which
have the two distinct rhyme-schemes required, while
there is no turn or change in the subject-matter of
the sestet from that of the octave. In such case they
are without any organic significance. They have
nothing to do with the constitution of the poem. The
poet has simply adopted the normal number of verses

[1] *The Westminster Review*, January, 1871, p. 78.
[2] 'Our Living Poets, An Essay in Criticism,' by H. Buxton Forman,
p. 209.

and the rhyme-schemes of a poetical art-structure, which are not called for by the character of his composition.

Tomlinson [1] gives the three types (according to the order of the rhymes) to which the greater number of the best Italian sonnets conform.

The rhyme-schemes of the three types are the following, those of the octaves being the same in all:

> Type I. *abbaabba   cdecde*
> Type II. *abbaabba   cdcdcd*
> Type III. *abbaabba   cdedce*

He shows that a large proportion of the sonnets of Petrarch, Dante, Michel Angelo, Tasso, Ariosto, and Vittoria Colonna, conform to one or other of these three types. The departures from them are chiefly the following:

A very small number of sonnets have their octaves in alternate rhyme: *abababab;* the rhymes of the second quatrain being sometimes reversed, *abab-baba.*

The exceptional rhyme-schemes of the sestets are the following:

> *cdecdc*
> *cdddcc*
> *cdeedc*
> *cdedec*
> *cdeccd*
> *cdeecd*

[1] 'The Sonnet: its Origin, Structure, and Place in Poetry. With original translations from the sonnets of Dante, Petrarch, etc., and remarks on the art of translating. By Charles Tomlinson, F.R.S.' London, John Murray, 1874.

But the number of sonnets whose sestets exhibit one or other of these exceptional rhyme-schemes is comparatively small.

After noting the metrical arrangements of 760 sonnets, by the above-named poets, he remarks: 'The conclusion to be drawn from these statements is, that the Italian sonnet is a poem of regular construction. It is not what some of our best English poets make it, namely, a short continuous poem, running through, from the first line to the last, in almost any order, and winding up with a couplet; but built up of parts or quatrains, the *Basi*, or bases, of the structure; and of tercets, or *Volte*, turnings or roads to which the *basi* point. Moreover, each quatrain has its peculiar office or function, as well as each tercet, and hence they should be kept distinct, and not be run into each other,—(as distinct as the separate parts of the Greek choral ode, which has been supposed by some to be the parent of the regular Italian sonnet;) the first quatrain being equivalent to the strophe, the second to the antistrophe; the first tercet to the epode, and the second tercet to the antipode.'

The great English poets who have most conformed to the normal Italian type, in the rhyme-schemes, and in observing a distinction in the functions of the octaves and the sestets, have not generally made the subdivisions of these (the quatrains and the tercets) distinct in function. This extreme of organic elaboration is not found in many English sonnets. It evidently does not suit the English genius. There is, it must be admitted, a certain

artistic satisfaction in such strictness of workmanship; but this strictness is more than compensated
for, in the greatest English sonnets, by the high
quality of the thought and feeling, in the two main
divisions, taken as wholes. When the functions of
these are kept distinct, there is an all-sufficient severity
of form. When this severity is carried further, the
danger is, if the subject-matter is not of a sufficiently
high quality, that of the result, when most successful,
may be said what Ovid says of the silver doors of
the palace of the Sun, '*materiem superabat opus*,' the
workmanship surpassed the material.

Matthew Arnold, in his Address as President of
the Wordsworth Society, 1883, after speaking of
Wordsworth's spiritual passion, when he is at his
highest, continues: 'A second invaluable merit which
I find in Wordsworth is this: he has something to
say. Perhaps one prizes this merit the more as one
grows old, and has less time left for trifling. Goethe
got so sick of the fuss about form and technical
details, without due care for adequate contents, that
he said if he were younger he should take pleasure
in setting the so-called art of the new school of poets
at naught, and in trusting for his whole effect to his
having something important to say.' [1]

---

[1] Eckermann, *Gespräche mit Goethe*, ii. 260–262: ' Es ist immer ein
Zeichen einer unproductiven Zeit, wenn die so ins Kleinliche des
Technischen geht, und eben so ist es ein Zeichen eines unproductiven
Individuums, wenn es sich mit dergleichen befasst . . . Wäre ich
noch jung und verwegen genug, so würde ich absichtlich gegen alle
solche technische Grillen verstossen . . . aber ich würde auf die
Hauptsache losgehen, und so gute Dinge zu sagen suchen, dass jeder
gereizt werden sollte, es zu lesen und auswendig zu lernen.'

There is not implied in these remarks any depreciation whatever of the importance of elaboration of form, without which, impassioned or spiritualized thought could not be adequately expressed. What is meant to be condemned is the mere *etiquette* of form, — a conventional, not an organic technique.

A number of sonnets will now be presented from Milton, Wordsworth, and other poets, which conform more or less strictly to the three Italian types, the octave rhyme-schemes of which are all *abba abba* called in Italian, *rima chiusa* (shut up or enclosed rhyme); and the sestet rhyme-schemes are: 1. *rima incatenata*, interlaced or interlocked rhymes, *cdc cdc* (variations of which are *cdc dcc* and *cdc ccd*); 2. *rima alternata*, alternate rhymes, *cdc dcd*.

Type I. *ABBA ABBA CDE CDE.*

This is regarded as the truest Italian type, and it certainly conforms best with the *idea* of the sonnet. The interlaced or interlocked rhymes of the sestet are the best adapted to what is the proper function of this division of the sonnet; for the reason that the rhyme-emphasis of this scheme is the most evenly distributed, each verse on which a rhyme falls being a third verse from that with which it rhymes. The quieter the subsidence of the thought and feeling in the sestet, the more agreeable the final impression generally is. Adjacent rhymes present a more or less sensible check to this subsidence, whether they close or are within the sestet.

To Cyriack Skinner. (Milton.)

Cyriack, whose grandsire [1] on the royal bench
   Of British Themis,[2] with no mean applause,
   Pronounced, and in his volumes taught, our laws,
   Which others at their bar so often wrench;
To-day deep thoughts resolve with me to drench
   In mirth that, after, no repenting draws;
   Let Euclid [8] rest, and Archimedes pause,
   And what the Swede intend,[4] and what the French.
To measure life learn thou betimes, and know
   Toward solid good what leads the nearest way;
   For other things mild Heaven a time ordains,
And disapproves that care, though wise in show,
   That with superfluous burden loads the day,
   And, when God sends a cheerful hour, refrains.

' Many of Wordsworth's so-called sonnets,' says Tomlinson, ' are not sonnets at all, according to the Italian definition; but it must also be added, that whenever he submits to that definition, whether consciously or not, and has some respect for the harmony of the form, the thought becomes more sharply defined and elaborated, and the result is not only Wordsworth's best sonnet, but an English sonnet deserving of the name. If I were called upon to justify this statement by an example, I should be disposed to cite the sonnet to Haydon. It is regularly

---

[1] Whose grandsire: Sir Edward Coke, Chief Justice of England. Skinner's mother was a daughter of Sir Edward.

[2] Themis: the goddess of law and justice.

[8] Skinner was fond of mathematical studies.

[4] Intend (ed. 1673): what the Swede and what the French intend. The Swede, Charles X. (Charles Gustavus), was carrying on war with Poland, and the French with the Spaniards in the Netherlands.

built up according to the first type — the second
quatrain terminates in a full point, and the tercets in
alternate rhyme[1] lead happily to a noble conclusion.'

To R. B. Haydon, Esq.

High is our calling, Friend! — Creative Art
(Whether the instrument of words she use,
Or pencil pregnant with ethereal hues)
Demands the service of a mind and heart,
Though sensitive, yet, in their weakest part
Heroically fashioned — to infuse
Faith in the whispers of the lonely Muse,
While the whole world seems adverse to desert.
And, oh, when Nature sinks, as oft she may,
Through long-lived pressure of obscure distress,
Still to be strenuous for the bright reward,
And in the soul admit of no decay,
Brook no continuance of weak-mindedness —
Great is the glory, for the strife is hard![2]

Four of the six beautiful sonnets which Longfellow
prefixed to his translation of Dante's ' Divina Com-

---

[1] The rhymes of the tercets are not alternate but interlaced or interlocked, *cde cde.*

[2] Sending this sonnet to Haydon on December 21, 1815, Wordsworth said it 'was occasioned, I might say inspired, by your last letter.' In Haydon's letter of November 27, the following occurs: " I
have benefited and have been supported in the troubles of life by your
poetry. I will bear want, pain, misery, and blindness; but I will never
yield one step I have gained on the road I am determined to travel
over.' *Prof. Knight's Note.* ' No new books worth sending for but
" Haydon's Life," which is as pathetic and strange as Rousseau's.' —
R. M. Milnes's Letter to C. J. MacCarthy, Oct. 18th, 1853.

media '[1] belong to Type I. The following is the second of the two prefixed to the 'Inferno.'

The Divina Commedia is conceived of as a vast minster, with its sculptures and statues, and elaborate emblematic devices, which uprose from the poet's agonies and exultations, his tenderness, his hate of wrong.

> How strange the sculptures that adorn these towers!
>   This crowd of statues, in whose folded sleeves
>   Birds build their nests ; while canopied with leaves
>   Parvis and portal bloom like trellised bowers,
> And the vast minster seems a cross of flowers!
>   But fiends and dragons on the gargoyled eaves
>   Watch the dead Christ between the living thieves,
>   And, underneath, the traitor Judas lowers!
> Ah! from what agonies of heart and brain,
>   What exultations trampling on despair,
>   What tenderness, what tears, what hate of wrong,
> What passionate outcry of a soul in pain,
>   Uprose this poem of the earth and air,
>   This mediæval miracle of song!

The following is the second of the two prefixed to the 'Purgatorio.' This sonnet is in the strictest accordance with the Italian type. Each quatrain and each tercet is distinct and has its own function. There are no sonnets in the language more perfect than this in their workmanship, nor more perfect, æsthetically. The rhyme-effect could not be finer, especially that from the vowel $\bar{e}$, in the sestet.

[1] The two examples of Type I., and the one example of Type II., are given with the kind permission of the publishers, Messrs. Houghton, Mifflin & Co., of Boston.

With snow-white veil and garments as of flame,
  She stands before thee, who so long ago
  Filled thy young heart with passion and the woe
  From which thy song and all its splendors came ;
And while with stern rebuke she speaks thy name,
  The ice about thy heart melts as the snow
  On mountain heights, and in swift overflow
  Comes gushing from thy lips in sobs of shame.
Thou makest full confession ; and a gleam,
  As of the dawn on some dark forest cast,
  Seems on thy lifted forehead to increase :
Lethe and Eunoe — the remembered dream
  And the forgotten sorrow — bring at last
  That perfect pardon which is perfect peace.

TYPE II. *ABBA ABBA CDC DCD.*

When the Assault was intended to the City.[1] (MILTON.)

Captain, or Colonel,[2] or Knight in Arms,
Whose chance on these defenceless doors may seize,
If deed of honour did thee ever please,[3]
Guard them, and him within protect from harms.

[1] '" *On his dore when ye citty expected an assault*" is the original heading of the sonnet in the copy of it, by an amanuensis, among the Cambridge MSS., as if the sonnet had actually been posted or nailed up on the outside of Milton's door. This title was afterwards deleted by Milton himself, and the other title substituted in his own hand; but the sonnet appeared without any title at all in the editions of 1645 and 1673.' — MASSON.

[2] Colonel: to be pronounced in three syllables, col-o-nel. 'Also spelt *coronel*, Holland's " Pliny," bk. xxii. c. 23; which is the Spanish form of the word, due to substitution of *r* for *l*, a common linguistic change; whence also the present pronunciation *curnel*.' — SKEAT's *Etymological Dictionary*.

[3] As it stands in the edition of 1673, and also in the Cambridge MS.; in the edition of 1645 it stands: ' If ever deed of honour did thee please.'

He can requite thee : for he knows the charms [1]
That call fame on such gentle acts as these,
And he can spread thy name o'er lands and seas,
Whatever clime the sun's bright circle warms.
Lift not thy spear against the Muses' bower :
The great Emathian [2] conqueror bid spare
The house of Pindarus, when temple and tower
Went to the ground ; and the repeated air [3]
Of sad [4] Electra's poet had the power
To save the Athenian walls from ruin bare.

Wordsworth's beautiful sonnet, 'The world is too much with us,' is in almost strict accordance with the second Italian type — the exception being that the subject-matter of the octave runs over into the ninth verse, but only to the extent of 2 *xa*, ' It moves us not,' and this transgression does not in the least impair the artistic merit of the sonnet. It rather has a pleasant effect, when the sonnet is read aloud. And then the transition to the sestet is distinctly marked by the exclamation, 'Great God! I'd rather be,' etc.

[1] Charms : magic verses, *carmina.* 'Carmina vel cælo possunt deducere lunam.' — VIRG. *Buc.* viii. 69 (Keightley).

[2] The great Emathian (Macedonian) conqueror : Alexander the Great, by whom Thebes was sacked, B.C. 333.

[3] And the repeated air : Plutarch tells us that when it was under debate in the camp of Lysander whether Athens should be levelled or not, a Phocian minstrel chanced to sing, at a banquet of the chief officers, the chorus from the ' Electra ' of Euripides, commencing with

Ἀγαμέμνονος ὦ κόρα,

ἤλυθον, Ἠλέκτρα, ποτὶ σὰν ἀγρότειραν αὐλάν, κ.τ.λ. *v.* 167,

and the guests were so affected that they declared it would be an unworthy deed to reduce to ruin a place so renowned as the birthplace of illustrious men. — repeated, *i.e.* recited, sung. — KEIGHTLEY.

[4] Sad : qualifies Electra.

The thought that our hearts are divorced from Nature, and her ministrations, is set forth in the first quatrain, and enforced by special instances, in the second — the two quatrains putting the reader in full and distinct possession of it.   In the sestet, the poet expresses his preference for a heart open to the consoling and cheering influences of the great mother, even if it were the heart of a pagan, having faith in the Nature-deities of Greece and Rome.

This sonnet ranks with the noblest in the literature, both in its matter and in its æsthetic merit.   The last two verses are grandly melodious.

> The world is too much with us; late and soon,
> Getting and spending, we lay waste our powers;
> Little we see in Nature that is ours;
> We have given our hearts away, a sordid boon!
> This Sea that bares her bosom to the moon;
> The winds that will be howling at all hours,
> And are up-gathered now like sleeping flowers;
> For this, for everything, we are out of tune;
> It moves us not. — Great God! I'd rather be
> A Pagan suckled in a creed outworn;
> So might I, standing on this pleasant lea,
> Have glimpses that would make me less forlorn
> Have sight of Proteus rising[1] from the sea;
> Or hear old Triton blow his wreathèd horn.

The following is the first of the two sonnets prefixed to Longfellow's translation of the 'Inferno':

> Oft have I seen at some cathedral door
>   A laborer, pausing in the dust and heat,
>   Lay down his burden, and with reverent feet
> Enter, and cross himself, and on the floor
> Kneel to repeat his paternoster o'er;

---

[1] Have sight of Proteus coming from the sea.   1807.

Far off the noises of the world retreat;
The loud vociferations of the street
Become an undistinguishable roar.
So, as I enter here from day to day,
And leave my burden at this minster gate,
Kneeling in prayer, and not ashamed to pray,
The tumult of the time disconsolate [1]
To inarticulate murmurs dies away,
While the eternal ages watch and wait.

TYPE III.   *ABBA ABBA CDE DCE.*

On his being arrived at the age of twenty-three.   (MILTON.)

How soon hath time, the subtle thief of youth,
Stolen on his wing my three and twentieth year!
My hasting days fly on with full career,
But my late spring no bud or blossom shew'th.[2]
Perhaps my semblance might deceive the truth,[3]
That I to manhood am arrived so near,
And inward ripeness doth much less appear
That some more timely happy spirits endu'th.
Yet be it less or more, or soon [4] or slow,
It shall be still in strictest measure even [5]
To that same lot [6] however mean or high,
Toward which time leads me and the will of heaven.
All is,[7] if I have grace to use it so,
As ever in my great taskmaster's eye.

[1] The reference here is, perhaps, to our Civil War.

[2] Shew'th: to be pronounced *shooth*.

[3] He appeared younger than he really was.   In his Second Defence of the people of England, he says: 'Though I am more than forty years old, there is scarcely any one to whom I do not appear ten years younger than I am.'

[4] Soon: adj. *early*.

[5] Still: *ever;* even: *equal in proportion.*

[6] Lot: *station in life.*

[7] All is, etc.: All depends upon my employing it as feeling myself to be under the eyes of my great Task-Master. — KEIGHTLEY.

Sonnets variously Irregular, but having the True Sonnet Character.

A number of sonnets will now be given which exhibit various departures from the normal Italian types, but which all realize, to a greater or less degree, the *idea* of the sonnet, and produce its peculiar artistic impression, more or less distinctly — that is, the impression derived from organic octave and sestet divisions, the octave division presenting, completely and distinctly, a basal thought or fact, from which proceeds, in the sestet, a corollary in the form of a sentiment, or reflection, or conclusion of some kind, such as would be suggested, by the thought or fact, to a flexible, and sensitive, and poetic mind. As has been just said, the sestet is a species of corollary, that is, a little crown or garland, as the word signifies, bestowed upon the thought in the octave.

The question to be asked, in judging what purports to be a sonnet, is, does it adequately meet the above conditions? It may not meet them, and yet be a very beautiful composition; but it is not a sonnet, in the strict special sense of the term.

The sonnets which follow illustrate the fact that the ideal type of the sonnet may be variously modified (not really departed from), and yet the distinctive character of the sonnet may be preserved, and its distinctive artistic effect produced. The Elizabethan sonnet cannot be said to be a modification of the sonnet proper, as its organic construction is different, and the resultant artistic effect is different

In the following sonnet, by Wordsworth, the octave rhyme-scheme is *abbabaab*, instead of the normal *abbaabba*, the *a's* and the *b's* being interchanged in the quatrains. Each quatrain is kept distinct, and has its own function — the first characterizing the rule-bound poet, the second advising a vital art which has its own inherent law, and follows it, regardless of outside and traditional authority and criticism.

The first tercet sets forth the freedom and boldness of the meadow-flower, in unfolding its bloom; the second represents the forest-tree as owing its grandeur to its own divine vitality.

This is a very pleasing sonnet.

A Poet! He hath put his heart to school,
Nor dares to move unpropped upon the staff
Which Art hath lodged within his hand — must laugh
By precept only, and shed tears by rule.
Thy Art be Nature: the live current quaff,
And let the groveller sip his stagnant pool,
In fear that else, when Critics grave and cool
Have killed him, Scorn should write his epitaph.
How does the Meadow-flower its bloom unfold?
Because the lovely little flower is free
Down to its root, and, in that freedom, bold;
And so the grandeur of the Forest-tree
Comes not by casting in a formal mould
But from its *own* divine vitality.

In the following sonnet, by Wordsworth, the rhyme-scheme of the octave is *ababcbcb*, the dominant and somewhat indistinct *b* rhyme (none, upon, tone, gone) imparting a tone well adapted to the theme. The turn which the thought takes in the sestet is in the

happiest manner of Wordsworth's sonnets. The
entire sonnet is very distinctly Wordsworthian in
thought and feeling.

> Most sweet is it with un-uplifted eyes
> To pace the ground, if path be there or none,
> While a fair region round the traveller lies
> Which he forbears again to look upon;
> Pleased rather with some soft ideal scene,
> The work of Fancy, or some happy tone
> Of meditation, slipping in between
> The beauty coming and the beauty gone.
> If Thought and Love desert us, from that day
> Let us break off all commerce with the Muse:
> With Thought and Love companions of our way,
> Whate'er the senses take or may refuse,
> The Mind's internal heaven shall shed her dews
> Of inspiration on the humblest lay.

Hood's beautiful sonnet, entitled 'Silence,' has a
most satisfying artistic effect; the artistic effect, too,
peculiar to the sonnet, notwithstanding that it ends
with a couplet. The couplet-rhyme, too, is a strong
one, falling, as it does, on a long *o*, encased, in both
rhyming words, in prolongable sub-vowels, *m*, *n*, and
l, *n*. But in this particular case, one would have to
be a bigoted stickler for the established legislation of
the sonnet, to condemn this violation of an important
sonnet rule. Rather, it must be felt that the final
word 'alone,' in itself, and also as emphasized by the
rhyme, contributes to the general impression aimed
after. The rhyme-scheme is *abbaabba cdcdee*.

In the octave, physical silence, if the expression be
allowed, is presented — the mere absence of all sound:
the silence of the grave, of the depths of the sea, of

the wide desert where no life is found; in the sestet, what may be called moral silence is presented — the silence which is deepened to the human spirit, and made 'self-conscious,' as it were, by human associations, and by sounds which intensify the sense of desolation.

The impression of solitude and silence is deepened by presenting to the mind green ruins and the desolate walls of antique palaces where man hath been, on the principle set forth by De Quincey, in his remarks on the effect of the expressions, 'amphitheatre of woods,' 'amphitheatre of hills': 'In the word *theatre* is contained an evanescent image of a great audience — of a populous multitude. Now this image — half withdrawn, half flashed upon the eye — and combined with the word *hills* or *forests*, is thrown into powerful collision with the silence of hills — with the solitude of forests; each image, from reciprocal contradiction, brightens and vivifies the other. The two images act and react, by strong repulsion and antagonism.' [1]

The sonnet, while being a beautiful composition in itself, is an admirable illustration of the functions of the two main divisions of the sonnet, — the sestet crowning the thought presented in the octave, — anointing it, so to speak.

> There is a silence where hath been no sound,
> There is a silence where no sound may be,
> In the cold grave — under the deep, deep sea,
> Or in wide desert where no life is found,

[1] 'Theological Essays and Other Papers,' Boston, 1860, vol ii. Milton, p. 108.

Which hath been mute, and still must sleep profound ;
No voice is hushed — no life treads silently,
But clouds and cloudy shadows wander free,
That never spoke, over the idle ground :
But in green ruins, in the desolate walls
Of antique palaces, where man hath been,
Though the dun fox, or wild hyæna, calls,
And owls that flit continually between,
Shriek to the echo, and the low winds moan,
There the true Silence is, self-conscious and alone.

Some readers might regard the last verse as an alexandrine ; but, in effect, when properly read, it is a pentameter verse. The voice should make a downward wave upon ' true,' the new idea, should go up on ' Silence is,' and down on the syllable ' con '; the last foot, ' alone,' should be read on a lower key, and the voice should be well filled out upon it.

Wordsworth's sonnet on Milton, written in London, September, 1802, is one of his noblest sonnets.

The poet invokes his great predecessor on the throne of English poetry, as one whose lofty spirit England needs, to lift her out of the base materialistic and utilitarian interests, the commonplace worldliness, in which she is absorbed, and to inspire her with nobler aims.[1] This is the basal thought presented in the octave — an octave remarkable for the closely packed

[1] The Rev. F. W. Robertson, in a lecture on Wordsworth, 1853, remarks that the first qualification for appreciating poetry is unworldliness, and adds : ' By worldliness I mean entanglement in the temporal and visible. It is the spirit of worldliness which makes a man love show, splendor, rank, title, and sensual enjoyments ; and occupies his attention, chiefly or entirely, with conversation respecting merely passing events, and passing acquaintances.'

elements included in its structure. And the many pauses required in its vocal expression, serve to exhibit the strong fervor of the invocation. For the proper reading of it, at least nineteen pauses are required. The quatrains are not kept distinct. In the sestet, the invocation is justified by the exalted character presented of the invoked, the sense of which is registered in the versification of the first tercet, which has a grandeur of movement, and there is a certain charm in the subsidence of that grandeur in the second tercet. The rhyme-scheme is *abbaabba cddcce.*

> Milton! thou shouldst be living at this hour:
> England hath need of thee: she is a fen
> Of stagnant waters: altar, sword, and pen,
> Fireside, the heroic wealth of hall and bower,
> Have forfeited their ancient English dower
> Of inward happiness. We are selfish men;
> Oh! raise us up, return to us again;
> And give us manners, virtue, freedom, power.
> Thy soul was like a Star, and dwelt apart:
> Thou hadst a voice whose sound was like the sea: [1]
> Pure as the naked heavens, majestic. free,
> So didst thou travel on life's common way,
> In cheerful godliness; and yet thy heart
> The lowliest duties on herself did lay.

In connection with this sonnet, the following, which is addressed to Coleridge, should be read. It was also written in London, September, 1802, and was

[1] O mighty-mouthed inventor of harmonies,
O skilled to sing of Time or Eternity,
God-gifted organ-voice of England,
Milton, a name to resound for ages.

       – TENNYSON.

prompted by the same state of things. The rhyme-scheme is the same: *abbaabba cddecc*. Though the matter of the first quatrain runs over, one foot ('Or groom') into the second quatrain, and the matter of the second quatrain into the first tercet, one foot and a light syllable, *xax* ('Delights us'), each quatrain and each tercet has its own function, and the full artistic effect of the sonnet organization is produced. Wordsworth seems to have been fond of this running over, a foot or two, of one division of the sonnet into another, and the effect is often good. It is so in this sonnet addressed to Coleridge:

> O Friend! I know not which way I must look
> For comfort, being, as I am, opprest,
> To think that now our Life is only drest
> For show: mean handy-work of craftsman, cook,
> Or groom! — We must run glittering like a Brook
> In the open sunshine, or we are unblest:
> The wealthiest man among us is the best:
> No grandeur now in nature or in book
> Delights us. Rapine, avarice, expense,
> This is idolatry: and these we adore:
> Plain living and high thinking are no more:
> The homely beauty of the good old Cause
> Is gone; our peace, our fearful innocence,
> And pure religion breathing household laws.

The last four verses are noble in sentiment and beautiful in expression. 'Plain living and high thinking,' and 'pure religion breathing household laws,' have become familiar quotations.

In a letter to Alexander Dyce (1833), Wordsworth writes: '. . . Though I have written so many [sonnets], I have scarcely made up my own mind upon the subject. It should seem that the sonnet, like any other legitimate composition, ought to have a beginning, a middle, and an end; in other words, to consist of three parts, like the three propositions of a syllogism, if such an illustration may be used. But the frame of metre adopted by the Italian does not accord with this view; and, as adhered to by them, it seems to be, if not arbitrary, best fitted to a division of the sense into two parts, of eight and six lines each. Milton, however, has not submitted to this; in the better half of his sonnets the sense does not close with the rhyme at the eighth line, but overflows into the second portion of the metre. Now, it has struck me, that this is not done merely to gratify the ear by variety and freedom of sound, *but also to aid in giving that pervading sense of intense unity in which the excellence of the sonnet has always seemed to me mainly to consist.* Instead of looking at this composition as a piece of architecture, making a whole out of three parts, I have been much in the habit of preferring the image of an orbicular body, — a sphere or a dew-drop. All this will appear to you a little fanciful; and I am well aware that a sonnet will often be found excellent, where the beginning, the middle, and the end are distinctly marked, and also where it is distinctly separated into *two* parts, to which, as I before observed, the strict Italian model, as they write it, is favorable. Of this last construction of sonnets, Russell's upon " Philoctetes " is a fine specimen; the first eight lines give the hardship of the case, the six last the consolation, or the *per contra.*'

What is italicized, in the above quotation, makes

it appear quite evident that Wordsworth often advisedly ran the subject-matter of the octave over into the sestet, for the purpose stated;[1] but whether that purpose was always secured thereby, is questionable. At any rate, where the subject-matter of the octave runs over into the sestet a foot or two, the true sonnet effect is not sensibly marred, as can be seen by some of the sonnets presented.

On the Lord General Fairfax at the Siege of Colchester.
(MILTON.)

abbaabba cddcdc

Fairfax, whose name in arms through Europe rings,
Filling each mouth with envy or with praise,
And all her jealous monarchs with amaze,
And rumours loud that daunt remotest kings;
Thy firm unshaken virtue[2] ever brings

---

[1] See the sonnets beginning with the following lines: 'Festivals have I seen that were not names'; 'Toussaint, the most unhappy man of men'; 'Great men have been among us; hands that penned'; 'It is not to be thought of that the Flood'; 'There is a bondage worse, far worse, to bear'; 'Nuns fret not at their convent's narrow room'; 'Fond words have oft been spoken to thee, Sleep'; 'Among the mountains were we nursed, loved Stream'; 'Dear to the Loves, and to the Graces vowed.' In the following, the subject-matter ends within the eighth verse: 'Is it a reed that's shaken by the wind'; 'Degenerate Douglas! oh, the unworthy Lord'; 'Six thousand veterans practised in war's game'; 'Clarkson! it was an obstinate hill to climb.' There are numerous others of this kind. In the sonnet, beginning 'I watch, and long have watched, with calm regret,' the octave subject-matter extends through the ninth verse, and yet the true sonnet effect is not entirely marred, though objection may be made to including the ninth verse in another rhyme-scheme.

[2] Virtue: *valor*, and there is also implied in the word Fairfax's purity of life. Milton pronounced a eulogy upon Fairfax, in his 'Second Defence of the People of England': 'Nor would it be

Victory home, though new rebellions raise
Their Hydra heads, and the false North[1] displays
Her broken league to imp their serpent-wings.
O yet a nobler task awaits thy hand
(For what can war but endless war still breed?)
Till truth and right from violence be freed,
And public faith cleared from the shameful brand
Of public fraud. In vain doth valour bleed,
While avarice and rapine share the land.

To Catherine Wordsworth. (WORDSWORTH.)

abbaacca dedede

Surprised by joy — impatient as the Wind
I turned to share the transport — Oh! with whom
But thee, deep buried in the silent Tomb,
That spot which no vicissitude can find?

right to pass over the name of Fairfax, who united the utmost fortitude with the utmost courage; and the spotless innocence of whose
life seemed to point him out as the peculiar favorite of Heaven.
Justly, indeed, may you be excited to receive this wreath of praise;
though you have retired as much as possible from the world, and
seek those shades of privacy which were the delight of Scipio. Nor
was it only the enemy whom you subdued, but you have triumphed
over that flame of ambition and that lust of glory which are wont to
make the best and the greatest of men their slaves. The purity of
your virtues and the splendor of your actions consecrate those sweets
of ease which you enjoy, and which constitute the wished-for haven
of the toils of man. . . . But whether it were your health, which I principally believe, or any other motive which caused you to retire, of
this I am convinced, that nothing could have induced you to relinquish
the service of your country, if you had not known that in your suc-
cessor liberty would meet with a protector, and England with a stay
to its safety, and a pillar to its glory' (Translation by Robert Fellowes).

[1] And the false North: the English Parliament affected to regard
the entrance of Hamilton's army into England in support of the Royal
cause as a breach of the Solemn League and Covenant between the
two nations. *Displays*, etc.: it would seem as if in poetic vision he
beheld the North spreading out a copy of the Covenant she had broken,

Love, faithful love recalled thee to my mind —
But how could I forget thee? — through what power,
Even for the least division of an hour,
Have I been so beguiled as to be blind
To my most grievous loss? — That thought's return
Was the worst pang that sorrow ever bore,
Save one, one only, when I stood forlorn,
Knowing my heart's best treasure was no more ;
That neither present time, nor years unborn
Could to my sight that heavenly face restore.

Tomlinson says of this sonnet that it ' has a strong Petrarchan flavour. Although loose in structure, it reads like a good, but free, translation of one of the early sonnets in the *Morte.*' By ' loose in structure,' he probably means that the subject-matter of the octave runs over into the ninth verse. That of the sestet begins with the fourth foot of the ninth verse. This looseness of structure does not, however, sensibly impair the true sonnet impression or effect. The same may be said of the concluding sonnet of the series on the River Duddon, entitled ' Afterthought,' in which the subject-matter of the octave runs over three feet and a light syllable ($3.xa+x$) into the ninth verse. Verily, this sonnet 'justifies its own structural form.' Matthew Arnold, in his Address as President of the Wordsworth Society, 1883, says: ' Milton was, of course, a far greater artist than Wordsworth ; probably, also, a greater force. But the spiritual passion when, as in the magnificent sonnet of farewell to the River Duddon,

to be cut up to *imp* the wings of the Hydra of rebellion. *Imp* is to graft; and in falconry, to imp a hawk's wing was to piece its broken feathers (KEIGHTLEY).

for instance, he is at his highest, and "sees into the life of things," cannot be matched from Milton. I will not say it is beyond Milton, but he has never shown it.'

The rhyme-scheme is *abbaabba cddcdc.*

I thought of Thee, my partner and my guide,
As being past away. — Vain sympathies!
For, backward, Duddon! as I cast my eyes,[1]
I see what was, and is, and will abide ;
Still glides the Stream, and shall not cease to glide ;
The Form remains, the Function never dies ;
While we. the brave, the mighty, and the wise,
We Men, who in our morn of youth defied
The elements, must vanish ; — be it so!
Enough, if something from our hands have power
To live, and act, and serve the future hour ;
And if, as toward the silent tomb we go,
Through love, through hope, and faith's transcendent dower,
We feel that we are greater than we know.[2]

To Mr. Lawrence.[3] (MILTON.)

abbaabba cdcced.

Lawrence,[4] of virtuous father virtuous son,
Now that the fields are dank, and ways are mire,
Where shall we sometimes meet, and by the fire

---

[1] Mr. A. J. George, in his 'Selections from Wordsworth,' p. 417, says, ' It is not possible to ascertain from what point the Poet took this view of the Duddon.' But 'backward as I cast my eyes' evidently means, as I look backward *in time.*

[2] 'And feel that I am happier than I know.' — *Paradise Lost,* viii. 282.

[3] 'A pleasing picture of the British Homer in his Horatian hour.' — RICHARD GARNETT.

[4] Lawrence : Henry Lawrence, son of the President of Cromwell's Council.

Help waste a sullen day, what may be won [1]
From the hard season gaining? Time will run [2]
On smoother, till Favonius [3] reinspire
The frozen earth, and clothe in fresh attire
The lily and rose that neither sowed nor spun.
What neat repast shall feast us, light and choice,
Of Attic taste, with wine, whence we may rise
To hear the lute well touched, or artful voice
Warble immortal notes and Tuscan air?
He who of those delights can judge, and spare [4]
To interpose them oft, is not unwise.

The octave material of the following sonnet by Milton runs over very effectively into the ninth verse, 3.*ra* ('And Worcester's laureate wreath'). The sestet rhyme-scheme (*cddcec*), including two sets of adjacent rhymes, would, in most cases, especially if the rhymes were on broad vowels, be objectionable, as checking too much the equable subsidence which the sestet should generally have; but the first, 'victories,' 'arise,' is hardly felt as a rhyme, and the strong rhyme-emphasis upon 'maw,' brings out as a final motived effect the holy indignation of the poet. The sonnet is signally Miltonic in its moral loftiness.

---

[1] **What may be, etc.:** gaining whatever may be won from the hard season.

[2] Time, in this way, will run on smoother for us, etc.

[3] Favonius: the Zephyr, or West-wind (a favendo vel fovendo).

[4] Spare: *refrain.* Keightley mistakes the meaning, in his note; he supplies 'time' after 'spare'; but the meaning is, he who can judge of those delights, and, at the same time, can refrain from interposing them oft in his occupations, is not unwise.

> Being mov'd, he will not spare to gird the gods.
>
> — *Coriolanus,* i. 1. 260.

To the Lord General Cromwell, May, 1652, on the pro-
posals of certain ministers at the committee for propaga-
tion of the Gospel.

> Cromwell, our chief of men, who through a cloud
>> Not of war only, but detractions rude,
>> Guided by faith and matchless fortitude,
> To peace and truth thy glorious way hast ploughed,
> And on the neck of crownèd Fortune proud
>> Hast reared God's trophies, and his work pursued.
> While Darwen [1] stream, with blood of Scots imbrued,
> And Dunbar field,[2] resounds thy praises loud,
> And Worcester's laureate wreath: yet much remains
>> To conquer still; Peace hath her victories
>> No less renowned than War: new foes arise,
> Threatening to bind our souls with secular chains.
>> Help us to save free conscience from the paw
>> Of hireling wolves,[3] whose Gospel is their maw.

'The effectiveness of Milton's sonnets,' says Mark
Pattison, 'is chiefly due to the *real* nature of the
character, person, or incident of which each is the
delineation. Each person, thing, or fact, is a moment in Milton's life, on which he was stirred; sometimes in the soul's depths, sometimes on the surface
of feeling, but always truly moved. He found the
sonnet enslaved to a single theme, that of unsuccess-

---

[1] Darwen stream: where Cromwell defeated an army of Scottish
royalists under the Duke of Hamilton, in August, 1648. See 'Cromwell's Letters and Speeches,' edited by Carlyle, Letter 64.

[2] Cromwell gained a great victory over the Scottish army at Dunbar,
September 3, 1650, and a decisive victory over the royal army, at Worcester, September 3, 1651. 'After a long flow of perspicuous and
nervous language, the unexpected pause at "Worcester's laureate
wreath," is very emphatical and has a striking effect.' — THOMAS
WARTON.

[3] Hireling wolves: the Presbyterian clergy is here meant.

ful love, mostly a simulated passion. He emancipated it, and as Landor says, "gave the notes to glory." And what is here felt powerfully, is expressed directly and simply. . . . It is a man who is speaking to us, not an artist attitudinizing to please us.'

And Lord Macaulay, in his ' Essay on Milton,' says of the sonnets: ' Traces, indeed, of the peculiar character of Milton, may be found in all his works; but it is most strongly displayed in the sonnets. Those remarkable poems have been undervalued by critics who have not understood their nature. They have no epigrammatic point. There is none of the ingenuity of Filicaja[1] in the thought, none of the hard and brilliant enamel of Petrarch in the style. They are simple but majestic records of the feelings of the poet, as little tricked out for the public eye as his diary would have been. A victory, an expected attack upon the City, a momentary fit of depression or exultation, a jest thrown out against one of his books, a dream which for a short time restored to him that beautiful face over which the grave had closed forever, led him to musings which, without effort, shaped themselves into verse. The unity of sentiment and severity of style which characterize these little pieces, remind us of the Greek Anthology, or perhaps still more of the Collects of the English Liturgy. The noble poem on the massacres of Piedmont is strictly a collect in verse.'

---

[1] An Italian lyric poet, born in Florence in 1642, and died there in 1707. Macaulay, in his ' Review of the Life and Writings of Addison,' speaks of him as ' a poet with whom Boileau could not sustain a comparison,' and as ' the greatest lyric poet of modern times.'

Byron's fine sonnet on Chillon has three rhymes in the octave, *abbaacca*, a new rhyme being introduced into the second quatrain instead of the regular *b* rhyme of the first. The rhymes of the sestet are alternate, *dedede*. There are but few sonnets in the literature which realize more distinctly the sonnet idea, or impart a fuller artistic satisfaction :

Eternal Spirit of the chainless Mind!
   Brightest in dungeons, Liberty! thou art,
   For there thy habitation is the heart —
The heart which love of thee alone can bind ;
And when thy sons to fetters are consigned —
   To fetters, and the damp vault's dayless gloom,
   Their country conquers with their martyrdom,
And Freedom's fame finds wings on every wind.
Chillon! thy prison is a holy place,
   And thy sad floor an altar — for 'twas trod,
Until his very steps have left a trace
Worn as if thy cold pavement were a sod,
By Bonnivard! May none those marks efface!
   For they appeal from tyranny to God.

The rhyme-scheme of the octave of the following sonnet by Wordsworth is the same as that of the preceding sonnet by Byron, *abbaacca*. The rhyme-scheme of the sestet is quite abnormal, *ddcffc*.

The rhyme *cc* is the same as the *aa* rhyme in the octave. This identity may have been accidental ; or the poet may have advisedly carried the *aa* rhyme into the sestet for a special artistic effect. It seems that he did.

The last verse of the octave and the last verse of the sestet both end with 'heard by thee' ; and the repetition is felt to be artistic. In the latter, the word 'neither' should be emphasized, and the voice should drift down on the remainder of the verse.

As has been said, an adjacent rhyme in the sestet, whether internal, or at the close, has not, generally, a good effect, as its emphasis presents a check to the quiet subsidence of the thought in the sestet. In the sonnet before us the first two verses of the sestet rhyme together, and the emphasis which the rhyme imparts to the word 'left,' which really expresses the pivotal idea of the sonnet, is felt to be artistic, as is also the new double-rhyme in the second quatrain, 'striven,' 'driven.'

The structure of the sonnet is of the very highest artistic merit.

Thought of a Briton on the subjugation of Switzerland.

Two Voices are there : one is of the sea,
One of the mountains ; each a mighty Voice :
In both from age to age thou didst rejoice,
They were thy chosen music, Liberty !
There came a Tyrant,[1] and with holy glee
Thou fought'st against him ; but hast vainly striven :
Thou from thy Alpine holds at length art driven,
Where not a torrent murmurs, heard by thee.
Of one deep bliss thine ear hath been bereft :
Then cleave, Oh, cleave to that which still is left ;
For, high-souled Maid, what sorrow would it be
That Mountain floods should thunder as before,
And Ocean bellow from his rocky shore,
And neither awful Voice be heard by thee!

Mark Pattison, after defining what is regarded as the most perfect form of the sonnet, says : 'How far

---

[1] A Tyrant : Napoleon Bonaparte, who invaded Switzerland in 1802.

any given specimen may deviate from type without
ceasing to be a sonnet, is as impossible to decide as
it is in botany to draw the line between a variety and
a distinct species. Perhaps we may say that success
is the best test, and that a brilliant example justifies
its own structural form. Or we may look for legis-
lative sanction in consent, and demand compliance
with those rules which the majority of poets agree to
respect. " The mighty masters are a law unto themselves, and the validity of their legislation will be
attested and held against all comers by the splendour
of an unchallengeable success." '

Of this the above sonnet is a signal illustration.
The question in regard to any irregular sonnet
should be, does it realize successfully the *idea* and
the peculiar artistic effect of the normal type of this
poetic form ?

Mrs. Browning's ' Sonnets from the Portuguese.'

Of Mrs. Browning's forty-four exquisite ' Sonnets
from the Portuguese,' but three, namely, the first,
fourth, and thirteenth, can be said to realize, with
any distinctness, the *idea* and the peculiar artistic
effect of the sonnet proper. Though they all exhibit the rhyme-scheme of the Italian type, *abba abba
cdcdcd*, they do not exhibit, even in the loosest form,
the required organic divisions — they are not ' built
up of parts or quatrains, the *Basi*, or bases, of the
structure; and of tercets, or *Volte*, turnings or roads
to which the *basi* point.' In their rhyme-schemes,
they have taken on the exterior semblance of what

organically they are not. They are the most beautiful love-poems in the language, but they cannot be classed as sonnets. The three following, the twenty-eighth, the thirty-eighth, and the forty-second, of the series, are examples, extreme, perhaps, of their general character, with the three exceptions named.

My letters all dead paper, . . . mute and white ! —
And yet they seem alive and quivering
Against my tremulous hands which loose the string
And let them drop down on my knee to-night.
This said, . . . He wished to have me in his sight
Once, as a friend : this fixed a day in spring
To come and touch my hand . . . a simple thing,
Yet I wept for it ! — this, . . . the paper's light, . . .
Said, *Dear, I love thee :* and I sank and quailed
As if God's future thundered on my past :
This said *I am thine* — and so its ink has paled
With lying at my heart that beat too fast :
And this . . . O love, thy words have ill availed,
If, what this said, I dared repeat at last !

First time he kissed me, he but only kissed
The fingers of this hand wherewith I write,
And ever since it grew more clean and white, . . .
Slow to world-greetings . . . quick with its ' Oh, list,'
When the angels speak. A ring of amethyst
I could not wear here plainer to my sight,
Than that first kiss. The second passed in height
The first, and sought the forehead, and half missed,
Half falling on the hair. O beyond meed !
That was the chrism of love which love's own crown,
With sanctifying sweetness, did precede.
The third upon my lips was folded down
In perfect purple state ! since when, indeed,
I have been proud and said, ' My Love, my own.'

How do I love thee ? let me count the ways.
I love thee to the depth and breadth and height
My soul can reach, when feeling out of sight
For the ends of Being and Ideal Grace.
I love thee to the level of everyday's
Most quiet need, by sun and candlelight.
I love thee freely, as men strive for Right :
I love thee purely, as they turn from Praise :
I love thee with the passion put to use
In my old griefs, and with my childhood's faith ;
I love thee with a love I seemed to lose
With my lost saints, — I love thee with the breath,
Smiles, tears, of all my life ! — and, if God choose,
I shall but love thee better after death.

As there is no shift in the thought, in these compositions, after the eighth verse, they do not call for two distinct sets of rhyme-schemes, certainly not the rhyme-schemes of the sonnet. They are felt to be purely arbitrary. The three quatrains and a couplet of the Shakespearian sonnet would have suited better the general character of the 'Sonnets from the Portuguese.' They are, in fact, fourteen-verse stanzas, in a continuous treatment of the same theme — 'waves of a prolonged melody.'

The three above-named sonnets, the first, fourth, and thirteenth, of the series, which meet the conditions of the sonnet proper, are the following. Of the first, the subject-matter of the octave runs over into the ninth verse, ending with 'A shadow across me.' The fourth and the thirteenth are strictly regular, so strictly, that not only the octaves and sestets are distinct in function, but, what is not usual in English sonnets, their subdivisions, the quatrains and tercets,

are likewise so. The tercets of the thirteenth are,
however, united in grammatical construction, but
there is a shift in the thought.

I thought once how Theocritus had sung
Of the sweet years, the dear and wished-for years,
Who each one in a gracious hand appears
To bear a gift for mortals, old or young:
And, as I mused it in his antique tongue,
I saw in gradual vision through my tears,
The sweet, sad years, the melancholy years,
Those of my own life, who by turns had flung
A shadow across me. Straightway I was 'ware,
So weeping, how a mystic Shape did move
Behind me, and drew me backward by the hair:
And a voice said in mastery while I strove,
' Guess now who holds thee?'—' Death!' I said. But there,
The silver answer rang . . . . ' Not Death, but Love.'

Thou hast thy calling to some palace floor,
Most gracious singer of high poems! where
The dancers will break footing from the care
Of watching up thy pregnant lips for more.
And dost thou lift this house's latch too poor
For hand of thine? and canst thou think and bear
To let thy music drop here unaware
In folds of golden fulness at my door ?
Look up and see the casement broken in,
The bats and owlets builders in the roof!
My cricket chirps against thy mandolin.
Hush ! call no echo up in further proof
Of desolation ! there's a voice within
That weeps . . . as thou must sing . . . alone, aloof.

And wilt thou have me fashion into speech
The love I bear thee, finding words enough,
And hold the torch out, while the winds are rough,
Between our faces to cast light on each? –

I drop it at thy feet.   I cannot teach
My hand to hold my spirit so far off
From myself . . . me . . . that I should bring thee proof
In words, of love hid in me out of reach.
Nay, let the silence of my womanhood
Commend my woman-love to thy belief, —
Seeing that I stand unwon, however wooed,
And rend the garment of my life in brief,
By a most dauntless, voiceless fortitude,
Lest one touch of this heart convey its grief.

Shakespeare's Sonnets.

The so-called sonnets of Shakespeare, which consist of three quatrains (each with its distinct set of
alternate rhymes) and a couplet, are a law to themselves, and are entirely exempt from the legislation
of the sonnet proper.   The rhyme-scheme is, *abab
cdcd efef gg.*   The thought developed in the three
quatrains leads up to its consummation, or climax, or
application of some kind in the couplet, the concluding verse receiving the strongest rhyme-emphasis,
and clinching the whole.   There is often a shifting
of the thought in the third stanza, the couplet sum-
ming up all.   The artistic effect is always distinct
and satisfying — far more so than is that of loosely
constructed compositions which have taken on the
outward semblance of the sonnet proper, without
having its organic character.   Such sonnets, when
turned to after reading a number of Shakespeare's,
especially impress us as misbegotten.

XVIII.

Shall I compare thee to a summer's day?
Thou art more lovely and more temperate:

Rough winds do shake the darling buds of May,
And summer's lease hath all too short a date:
Sometime too hot the eye of heaven shines,
And often is his gold complexion dimmed;
And every fair from fair sometimes declines,
By chance or nature's changing course untrimmed;
But thy eternal summer shall not fade,
Nor lose possession of that fair thou owest,[1]
Nor shall death brag thou wander'st in his shade,
When in eternal lines to time thou grow'st:
  So long as men can breathe, or eyes can see,
  So long lives this, and this gives life to thee.

XXIX.

When, in disgrace with fortune and men's eyes,
I all alone beweep my outcast state,
And trouble deaf heaven with my bootless cries,
And look upon myself, and curse my fate,
Wishing me like to one more rich in hope,
Featured like him, like him with friends possessed,
Desiring this man's art, and that man's scope,
With what I most enjoy contented least;
Yet in these thoughts myself almost despising,
Haply I think on thee, and then my state,
Like to the lark at break of day arising
From sullen earth, sings hymns at heaven's gate:
  For thy sweet love remembered such wealth brings
  That then I scorn to change my state with kings.

XXX.

When to the sessions of sweet silent thought
I summon up remembrance of things past,
I sigh the lack of many a thing I sought,
And with old woes new wail my dear time's waste:
Then can I drown an eye, unused to flow,
For precious friends hid in death's dateless[2] night,

[1] That fair thou owest: that beauty thou possessest.
[2] Dateless: *endless.*

And weep afresh love's long since cancelled woe,
And moan the expense [1] of many a vanished sight:
Then can I grieve at grievances foregone,
And heavily from woe to woe tell o'er [2]
The sad account of fore-bemoanèd moan,
Which I new pay as if not paid before.
    But if the while I think on thee, dear friend,
    All losses are restored and sorrows end.

XXXIII.

Full many a glorious morning have I seen
Flatter the mountain tops with sovereign eye,
Kissing with golden face the meadows green,
Gilding pale streams with heavenly alchemy;
Anon permit the basest clouds to ride
With ugly rack on his celestial face,
And from the forlorn world his visage hide,
Stealing unseen to west with this disgrace:
Even so my sun one early morn did shine,
With all-triumphant splendour on my brow;
But, out, alack! he was but one hour mine,
The region cloud hath masked him from me now.
    Yet him for this my love no whit disdaineth;
    Suns of the world may stain [3] when heaven's sun
        staineth.

LV.

Not marble, nor the gilded monuments
Of princes, shall outlive this powerful rime:
But you shall shine more bright in these contents
Than unswept stone, besmeared with sluttish time.

---

[1] Moan the expense: Schmidt explains *expense* as loss, but does not
'moan the expense' mean *pay my account of moans for?* The words
are explained by what follows:

> *Tell o'er*
> *The sad account of fore-bemoanèd moan*
> *Which I new pay as if not paid before.* — DOWDEN.

[2] Tell o'er: *count over.*   [3] Stain: *become dim.*

When wasteful war shall statues overturn,
And broils root out the work of masonry,
Nor Mars his sword nor war's quick fire shall burn
The living record of your memory.
'Gainst death and all-oblivious enmity
Shall you pace forth ; your praise shall still find room
Even in the eyes of all posterity
That wear this world out to the ending doom.
   So, till the judgment that yourself arise,[1]
   You live in this, and dwell in lovers' eyes.

Spenser's Amoretti.

The Amoretti of Spenser consist, as do the sonnets of Shakespeare, of three quatrains and a couplet, but the quatrains are interlaced by the rhyme-scheme, it being *abab bcbc cdcd ee.* That is, the last rhyme of the first stanza is continued in the first and third verses of the second ; and the last rhyme of the second stanza is continued in the first and third verses of the third. This reiteration of rhymes contributes to the ardency of the expression ; but it is often felt to be too much of a good thing, especially when the rhymes are double or female rhymes.

Happy, ye leaves! when as those lilly hands,
Which hold my life in their dead-doing might,
Shall handle you, and hold in loves soft bands,
Lyke captives trembling at the victors sight.
And happy lines! on which, with starry light,
Those lamping[2] eyes will deigne sometimes to look,
And reade the sorrows of my dying spright,
Written with teares in harts close-bleeding book.

---

[1] Till the judgment that yourself arise : till the decree of the judgment day that you arise from the dead. — DOWDEN.

[2] Lamping : shining : — 'lamping sky' (*Faerie Queene,* 3. 3. 1).

And happy rymes! bathed in the sacred brooke
Of Helicon, whence she derivèd is;
When ye behold that Angels blessed looke,
My soules long-lackèd foode, my heavens blis:
  Leaves, lines, and rymes, seeke her to please alone,
  Whom if ye please, I care for other none!

When the Amoretti are read continuously, the
reader wearies of the 'volée de résonnance'; especially when the double or female rhymes come in, as
in the following:

Sweet Smile! the daughter of the Queene of Love,
Expressing all thy mothers powrefull art,
With which she wonts to temper angry Jove,
When all the gods he threats with thundering dart:
Sweet is thy vertue, as thy selfe sweet art.
For, when on me thou shinedst late in sadnesse,
A melting pleasance ran through every part,
And me revivèd with hart-robbing gladnesse.
Whylest rapt with joy resembling heavenly madnesse,
My soule was ravisht quite as in a traunce;
And feeling thence, no more her sorrowes sadnesse,
Fed on the fulnesse of that chearefull glaunce,
  More sweet than Nectar, or Ambrosiall meat,
  Seemd every bit which thenceforth I did eat.

Though the sonnet was introduced into English
literature by Henry Howard, Earl of Surrey,[1] it was
not until Milton used it, a hundred years later and
more, that the normal Italian type was followed with
any degree of strictness. 'Milton's distinction in the
history of the sonnet,' says Mark Pattison, 'is that,
not overawed by the great name of Shakespeare, he
emancipated this form of poem from the two vices

---

[1] Born about 1517; beheaded January 21, 1547.

which depraved the Elizabethan sonnet — from the
vice of misplaced wit in substance, and of misplaced
rime in form.   He recognized that the sonnet belonged
to the poetry of feeling, and not to the poetry of
ingenuity.   And he saw that the perfection of metrical construction was not reached by tacking together
three four-line verses rounded by a couplet at the
end.'

Pattison is hardly ·just here.   The sonnets of
Shakespeare, and other Elizabethan sonnets, should
be judged absolutely, and not relatively to the normal
type of the Italian sonnet.   The fact that they are
fourteen-verse compositions does not necessarily ren-
der them amenable to the legislation of the Italian
sonnet.   The question should be, have they their *own*
artistic effect?   Shakespeare's sonnets certainly have,
and, in general, a most satisfying artistic effect.   And
so have a large number of sonnets by Spenser and
other poets of the time.

Pattison continues: 'Milton had put his poetical
genius to school to the Italians, Dante, Petrarch, and
the rest.   What of art Milton could adopt from them,
he had appropriated.   The tradition of the sonnet,
coming from what had not ceased to be regarded as
the home of learning, appealed to his classical feeling.   His exquisite ear for rhythm dictated to him a
recurrence to the Italian type in the arrangement of
the rimes.   We may be sure that Milton's ungrudg-
ing submission to the rules of the sonnet was not
deference to authority.   To that arch-rebel, rule and
law were as a thread of tow, if they could not justify
themselves to reason.   Not so much the Italian tradi-

tion, as his own sense of fitness, made Milton recur
to the Italian type from which the sonnet had devi-
ated since its first introduction by Surrey.'

These remarks are quite acceptable. But they
are, after all, merely equivalent to saying that Milton
saw, in the constitution of the normal type of the
Italian sonnet, a form of poetic art which suited his
purpose, which form he felt at liberty to modify
somewhat, while, at the same time he secured, more
or less, its peculiar artistic effect. Whatever condemnation he might have pronounced upon the Elizabethan sonnet, as written by Shakespeare, Spenser,
Sidney, Daniel, and others, he certainly was not the
man to condemn it by reason of its deviations from
the Italian type. He would have condemned it, if at
all, on absolute principles, regarding it as an independent form of poetic art.

XI

GENERAL REMARKS ON BLANK VERSE.

THE crowning glory of English poetical and dramatic language-shaping is blank verse, in its most vital, organic forms — the forms developed in the Elizabethan era, and the epic form as produced by the 'mighty-mouthed inventor of harmonies,' the 'God-gifted organ-voice of England,' who could not, perhaps, with all his inborn power, have attained to such consummate and never-to-be-equalled excellence, had he not profited by the dramatic blank verse of Shakespeare and his contemporaries.

And there is no mode of language-shaping which exhibits such a variety of degrees of merit and of demerit. The worst and the best hardly admit of comparison, any more than things which have nothing in common. The only respect in which they may be said to agree is, that the metrical theme is 5.ra. The highest merits of blank verse can hardly be said to have any existence in the earliest attempts at this literary form, in which the verse has altogether its own way, so to speak, and the thought is forced to submit to that way. Its movement had been derived from rhyming verse, and could not readily be changed. Much, indeed, of the earlier blank verse, at its best, may be characterized as unrhymed couplet-verse; at its worst, it is but a succession of verses, each being, syntactically, an unconnected unit in the series.

. But such an imperfect medium of expression was not at all suitable for the great dramatic geniuses who were soon to appear, and by one of the earliest of whom, fortunately, the great capabilities of this medium of expression were to be recognized, and, to some degree, realized. The relations of the verse and the thought to be conveyed by it had to undergo an entire change. The thought was to have *its* own way, determine its own orbit, and the verse was, in its turn, to submit to that way.

The stages of the change can be quite distinctly traced, especially in Shakespeare. He began to write when the change had decidedly set in. The verse had learned to come into some submission to the dramatic thought which it had to convey. This submission Christopher Marlowe had taught it to some extent — to a very considerable extent — when Shakespeare took it in hand. And such was the plastic power of Shakespeare's thought that, in a few years, a complete submission was brought about, as is shown in his later plays, wherein the verse is as fully obedient to the thought as, before, the thought was to the verse. But for this change in their re-lations to each other, the English drama could not have been what it became, notwithstanding that there was more dramatic genius in England, at the time, than we have any record of in any previous period of human history.

The chances of the drama, too, would have been

still less if rhymed pentameter verse had become an established form. This form asserted itself, for a time, in the dreary Restoration Drama — in the 'heroic' plays of Dryden and others, which are 'full of sound and fury, signifying nothing.' The sound and fury took the place of honest vital thought and genuine unaffected feeling.

Shakespeare was evidently fond of rhyme, in the earlier period of his career; but as his dramatic identification advanced, rhyme had to give way, and in his latest plays there is very little of it. Blank verse became the only fitting organ for his dramatic genius in its most advanced development.

In the earliest blank verse in the language, that of Henry Howard, Earl of Surrey's translation of the second and fourth books of Virgil's 'Æneid,' done about 1540, and first published in 1557, the orbit of the thought is generally determined by the metre. There is but little *enjambement;* the sense is not, in Milton's words, 'variously drawn out from one verse into another.' One verse follows another with a dull uniformity. The ear dwells on the termination of the verse; the mind hovers within the limits of one verse, or of a couplet, at a time.

Nicholas Grimoald's blank verse,[1] first published in 'Tottell's Miscellany,' 1557, the same year in which Surrey's translations from Virgil were published, is superior to Surrey's. There is more spontaneity, more *go*, in it; and it does not show so much metre

---

[1] That of 'The Death of Zoroas, an Egyptian astronomer, who was killed in Alexander's first battle with the Persians,' and other pieces See Warton's 'History of English Poetry.'

consciousness as is always present in Surrey's. Warton remarks, in his ' History of English Poetry,' ' To
the style of blank verse exhibited in Surrey, he added
new strength, elegance, and modulation. In the
disposition and conduct of his cadencies, he often
approaches to the legitimate structure of the improved
blank verse.'

The first tragedy in blank verse was ' Gorboduc '
(or, ' Ferrex and Porrex '), the joint production of
Thomas Norton and Thomas Sackville. It was
acted before Queen Elizabeth, at Whitehall, in 1561.
Its blank verse, like that of Surrey, exhibits only
occasional shiftings of the regular accent, and extra
unaccented syllables; here and there an *enjambement*
and a broken verse; no excursions of the thought
from the metre; and though there are passages of
connected lines, each line is generally felt as a distinct
unit in the series.

It may be said that Marlowe did more in the way
of *indicating* the dramatic capabilities of blank verse,
by freeing it from some of the fetters in which it had
been bound, than of realizing those capabilities on
the higher planes of expression to which Shakespeare
carried them. He certainly did not do all that John
Addington Symonds credits him with, in his ' Shakespeare's Predecessors in the English Drama.'

There is not, generally, in his plays, that sanity of
mind and heart, that well-balanced and well-toned
thought and genuine passion, to have brought out
the higher capabilities of the verse.

The student could not be referred to any passage
in his plays, which would better serve, perhaps, to

represent his blank verse in its best estate, than the
first scene of the fifth act of his ' Edward the Second,'
in which the king, after his deposition, reluctantly
gives up his crown to the Bishop of Winchester and
the Earl of Leicester. The scene in Shakespeare's
' Richard the Second,' in which Richard is represented
under similar circumstances (4. 1. 162–318), should
be read in connection with this, for the purpose of
comparing Shakespeare's earlier blank verse with
Marlowe's best. The scene in ' Edward the Second,'
in which the king is put to death, the fifth of the
fifth act, also contains some of the best verse which
Marlowe wrote.

The blank verse of ' Tamburlaine ' is more high-
sounding, indeed, than that of ' Edward the Second ';
but it is in ' Ercles' vein, a tyrant's vein,' — pompous
and passionless. Thought and passion must be per-
fectly *honest*, in order to be subtly plastic. Tamburlaine and the Jew of Malta are monsters, in their
several ways; and much of what they are made to
say, ' o'ersteps the modesty of nature.' [1]

The work begun by Marlowe, of bringing blank
verse into a conformity with the demands of dramatic

---

[1] It should be remembered that the exaggeration of high-sounding
language of which Marlowe has been accused was, in part at least,
intentional, and was meant to supply some of the resonance that the
ear would miss in the absence of rhyme. This is plainly stated in the
prologue to ' Tamburlaine,' Part i. :

> From jigging veins of rhyming mother wits,
> And such conceit as clownage keeps in pay,
> We'll lead you to the stately tent of war,
> Where you shall hear the Scythian Tamburlaine,
> Threatening the world with high-astounding terms.

Osborne William Tancock's edition of Marlowe's ' Edward the
Second.' Introd., p. vi.

thought, was carried on and perfected by Shakespeare; and the evolution of this wonderful organ of
dramatic expression can be traced in his plays, from
a more or less monotonous alternation of unaccented
and accented syllables, the thought metre-bound or
couplet-bound, up to an operation of the perfect law
of liberty; the flexibility and the continuity of the
thought, and the vivacity and the fluctuations of the
feelings resulting in all manner of variations upon
the theme-forms, — shiftings of the regular rhythmical
accent, extra end-syllables, constant breaks in the
verse, weak endings of verses, upon which the voice
cannot press, but must move on without a pause, an
interweaving of verses and, as a consequence, a
sinking of the metre, to a greater or less extent,
accelerations and retardations of movement, which
way the thought and feeling sway it, etc., etc.

See the following passages: Love's Labor's Lost,
2. 1. 13–34; Two Gentlemen of Verona, 2. 7. 1–38;
Midsummer Night's Dream, 4. 1. 108–124; Richard
the Third, 1. 1. 1–41; Romeo and Juliet, 2. 2. 1–190;
3. 2. 1–31; 4. 1. 77–88; 4. 3. 36–58; King John, 3.
3. 19–55; 1 Henry IV., 1. 3. 1–302; 4. 1. 97–110;
Julius Cæsar, 3. 1. 254–275; 3. 2. 78–234; Troilus
and Cressida, 1. 3. 75–137; Hamlet, 1. 2. 129–159;
Othello, 1. 3. 158–168; 2. 3. 169–178; 3. 3. 347–
357; 451–460; 3. 4. 55–75; 4. 2. 47–64; 5. 2. 338–
356; King Lear, 1. 4. 318–332; 2. 4. 89–120; 4. 6.
11–24; Macbeth, 1. 5. 16–59; 4. 1. 48–61; Antony
and Cleopatra, 4. 14. 1–54; 5. 2. 76–92; Coriolanus,
3. 3. 120–135; Cymbeline, 3. 2. 50–70; Winter's
Tale, 1. 2. 1–465; 3. 2. 23–46; 176–203; 4. 4. 112–

129; Tempest, 1. 2. 1–501; 5. 1. 33–57. The numbering of the lines is that of the Globe Shakespeare.

Dramatic blank verse has never, perhaps, attained to more organic forms than are exhibited by the second scene of the first act of ' The Winter's Tale,' and the second scene of the first act of ' The Tempest.' These two scenes every student of Shakespeare should read again and again; should memorize, indeed, as the perfection, humanly speaking, of dramatic language-shaping.

XII.

MILTON'S BLANK VERSE.

THE two grand features of Milton's blank verse, are

1. The melodious variety of his cadences closing within verses ; this being one of the essentials of 'true musical delight' which Milton mentions, in his remarks on 'The Verse,' 'the sense variously drawn out from one verse into another'; and

2. The melodious and harmonious grouping of verses into what may, with entire propriety, be called stanzas [1] — stanzas which are more organic than the uniformly constructed stanzas of rhymed verse. The latter must be more or less artificial, by reason of the uniformity which is maintained. But the stanzas of Milton's blank verse are waves of harmony which are larger or smaller, and with ever-varied cadences, according to the propulsion of the thought and feeling which produces them, which propulsion may be sustained through a dozen verses or more, or may expend itself in two or three.

No other blank verse in the language exhibits such a masterly skill in the variation of its pauses — pauses, I mean, where periodic groups, or logical sections of groups, terminate, after, or within, it may be, the

[1] See note, p. 21.

first, second, third, or fourth foot of a verse. There are five cases where the termination is within the fifth foot.

The following table exhibits the various parts of verses, in the order of their numerical rank, after which pauses occur. The variations of the regular foot (*xa*), in these parts of verses, are also shown, the accented syllable being often shifted, and unaccented syllables being often added. These variations are not arbitrary, but, when properly read aloud, in their connection, will be found to be organic ; that is, they have a logical or an æsthetic significance. It has been seen, in a former chapter, how these variations were misunderstood and condemned by Dr Johnson and other critics of the eighteenth century.

3 *xa*	587
2 *xa* .	497
2 *xa* | *a*[1]	242
3 *xa* | *a*	198
xa | *x* .	184
4 *xa*	149
xa	116
ax | *xa*	78
ax | 2 *xa*	75
ax | *xa* | *x*	51
ax | 2 *xa* | *x*	26
ax	23
ax | 3 *xa*	18
2 *xa* | *ax*	15
2 *xa* | *xxa*	13
xa | *xxa* | *xa*	13
xa | *xxa*	8
xa | *ax*	8

[1] Wherever a final *x* or *xx* occurs, the *a* syllable follows the pause in the succeeding group or section of a group.

4 *xa* | *x*	5
2 *ax* | *xa*	5
axx | *xa*	4
a	4
xa | *xxa* | *x* .	4
ax | *xxa* | *xa* | *x* .	4
3 *xa* | *xx*	4
xax | 2 *xa*	2
ax | *xa* | *xxa*	2
xa | *xxa* | 2 *xa*	2
xxa | *xa*	2
ax | *x* .	1
xa | *xxa* | *xa* | *x* .	1
ax | *xxa*	1
ax | *xa* | *xx* .	1
xax	1
axx | 3 *xa*	1
axx | *ax*	1
ax | 2 *xa* | *xxa*	1
axx	1
ax | *xa* | *ax* | *xa* .	1
xxa | 2 *xa*	1
2 *xa* | *ax* | *xa*	1
ax | 3 *xa* | *x*	1
xa | *ax* | *x* .	1
xxa | *xa* | *x* .	1
xxa | *x*	1
xa | *ax*	1

Of the 2355 pauses, where periodic groups, or logical sections of groups, terminate, 587 (almost exactly one-fourth of the whole number) occur after 3 *xa*.[1] This section of verse may be regarded as a secondary metrical theme to the primary, 5 *xa*, other sections being, in their turn, variations upon this.

[1] The whole number of pauses after the third foot is 696, there being 75 (*ax* \| 2 *xa*), 13 (2 *xa* \| *xxa*), 13 (*xa* \| *xxa* \| *xa*), 5 (2 *ax* \| *xa*), 2 (*ax* \| *xa* \| *xxa*), and 1 (*xxa* \| 2 *xa*).

Examples of the Several Kinds of Pauses or Stops.

3 *xa* :

And chiefly Thou, O Spirit, that dost prefer
Before all temples the upright heart and pure.
Instruct me, for Thou know'st ;

—i. 19.

Or hear'st thou rather, pure ethereal stream,
Whose fountain who shall tell ?

— iii. 8.

So thick a drop serene hath quenched their orbs,
Or dim suffusion veiled.

— iii. 26.

On to their morning's rural work they haste,
Among sweet dews and flowers ;

— v. 212.

All night, the dreadless Angel, unpursued,
Through Heav'ns wide champain held his way, till morn,
Waked by the circling hours, with rosy hand
Unbarred the gates of light.

—vi. 4.

2 *xa* :

on his right
The radiant image of his glory sat,
His only Son :

— iii. 64.   .

Freely we serve,
Because we freely love, as in our will
To love or not :

— v. 540.

Others on silver lakes and rivers bathed
Their downy breast.

— vii. 438.

2 *xa* | *x* :

But if death
Bind us with after-bands, what profits the
Our inward freedom ?

>   where highest woods impenetrable
> To star or sun-light, spread their umbrage broad,
> And brown as ev'ning !

— ix. 1088.

> How didst thou grieve then, Adam, to behold
> The end of all thy offspring, end so sad,
> Depopulation !

— xi. 756.

3 *xa* | *x*:

>   his doom is fair,
> That dust I am, and shall to dust return.
> O welcome hour whenever !

— x. 771.

> His starry helm unbuckled showed him prime
> In manhood where youth ended.

— xi. 246.

>   others, whence the sound
> Of instruments, that made melodious chime,
> Was heard, of harp and organ ;

— xi. 560.

xa | *x*:

>   They astonished, all resistance lost,
> All courage ;

— vi. 839.

>   Hell saw
> Heav'n ruining from Heav'n, and would have fled
> Affrighted ;

— vi. 869.

> Her long with ardent look his eye pursued.
> Delighted ;

— ix. 398.

> Yet oft his heart, divine of something ill,
> Misgave him :

— ix. 846.

4 *xa* :

> These, lulled by nightingales, embracing, slept,
> And on their naked limbs the flow'ry roof
> Showered roses, which the morn repaired.

— iv. 773.

So under fiery cope together rushed
Both battles main, with ruinous assault
And inextinguishable rage.

— vi. 217.

They plucked the seated hills with all their load,
Rocks, waters, woods, and, by the shaggy tops
Uplifting, bore them in their hands.

— vi. 646.

xa :

So on this windy sea of land, the Fiend
Walked up and down alone, bent on his prey:
Alone :

— iii. 442.

the careful plowman doubting stands,
Lest on the threshing-floor his hopeful sheaves
Prove chaff.

— iv. 985.

He celebrated rode
Triumphant through mid Heav'n, into the courts
And temple of his Mighty Father throned
On high :

— vi. 891.

in his own image he
Created thee, in the image of God
Express ;

— vii. 528.

ax | xa :

Celestial tabernacles where they slept
Fanned with cool winds ;

— v. 655.

Saw where the sword of Michael smote, and felled
Squadrons at once :

— vi. 251

Unfeignèd Hallelujahs to thee sing
Hymns of high praise :

— vi 745.

And the third sacred morn began to shine
Dawning through Heav'n.

— vi. 749.

He on his impious foes right onward drove.
Gloomy as night :

— vi. 832.

that milky way,
Which nightly as a circling zone thou seest
Powdered with stars.

— vii. 581.

This is one of the most beautiful cadences in the
'Paradise Lost.'   See, also, vii. 631 ; viii. 314, 389 ; ix.
394, 434, 465, 578 ; x. 185, 304, 412, 789, 880 ; xi.
152, 240, 465, 495 ; xii. 537, etc.

ax | 2 *xa* :

The bold design
Pleased highly those infernal states, and joy
Sparkled in all their eyes.

— ii. 388.

On a green shady bank profuse of flow'rs,
Pensive I sat me down ;

— viii. 287.

for those
Appointed to sit there had left their charge,
Flown to the upper world ;

— x. 422.

Thus was the applause they meant
Turned to exploding hiss ;

— x. 546.

In th' midst an altar as the land-mark stood,
Rustic, of grassy sord.[1]

— xi. 433.

though here thou see him die
Rolling in dust and gore.

— xi. 460.

So may'st thou live till, like ripe fruit, thou drop
Into thy mother's lap, or be with ease
Gathered, not harshly plucked :

— xi. 537.

[1] Sward. Shakespeare's ' W. T.,' ' greene-sord ' (1st Folio), iv. 4. 157.

>   till in his rage
> Pursuing whom he late dismissed, the sea
> Swallows him with his host;
>
>   — xii. 196.

This is also a beautiful and very effective cadence.
It occurs seventy-five times.

ax | xa | x:

> Into this wild abyss the wary Fiend
> Stood on the brink of Hell and looked a while,
> Pond'ring his voyage;
>
>   — ii. 919.

> And in their motions harmony divine
> So smoothes her charming tones, that God's own ear
> Listens delighted.
>
>   — v. 627.

>   part huge of bulk
> Wallowing unwieldly, enormous in their gait,
> Tempest the ocean;
>
>   — vii. 412.

> With burnished neck of verdant gold, erect
> Amidst his circling spires, that on the grass
> Floated redundant.
>
>   — ix. 503.

>   nor stood much in awe
> Of man, but fled him, or with count'nance grim
> Glared on him passing.
>
>   — x. 714.

>   On the ground
> Outstretched he lay, on the cold ground, and oft
> Cursed his creation;
>
>   — x. 852.

>   High in front advanced,
> The brandished sword of God before them blazed
> Fierce as a comet;
>
>   — xii. 634.

ax | 2 xa | x:

>   who wont to meet
> So oft in festivals of joy and love
> Unanimous, as sons of one great sire
> Hymning th' Eternal Father;
>
>   — vi. 96.

Whence hail to thee,
Eve, rightly called mother of all mankind,
Mother of all things living;

— xi. 160.

a different sort
From the high neighb'ring hills, which were their seat,
Down to the plain descended.

— xi. 576.

those few escaped
Famine and anguish will at last consume,
Wand'ring that watery desert.

— xi. 779.

ax :

With parted spears, as thick as when a field
Of Ceres ripe for harvest waving bends
Her bearded grove of ears, which way the wind
Sways them;

— iv. 983.

nor is it aught but just
That he who in debate of truth hath won
Should win in arms, in both disputes alike
Victor;

— vi. 124.

who him defied,
And at his chariot-wheels to drag him bound
Threatened;

— vi. 359.

Thus they in lowliest plight, repentant, stood
Praying;

— xi. 2.

Studious they appear
Of arts that polish life, inventors rare,
Unmindful of their Maker, though his Spirit
Taught them;

— xi. 612.

ax | 3 *xa* :

Encroached on still through your intestine broils,
Weak'ning the sceptre of old Night:

— ii. 1002.

Yet not the more
Cease I to wander where the Muses haunt
Clear spring, or shady grove, or sunny hill,
Smit with the love of sacred song;

— iii. 29

All Heav'n,
And happy constellations on that hour
Shed their selectest influence!

— viii. 513.

As God in Heav'n
Is centre, yet extends to all, so thou
Centring receiv'st from all those orbs;

— ix. 109.

However, I with thee have fixed my lot,
Certain to undergo like doom.

— ix. 953

The voice of God they heard
Now walking in the garden, by soft winds
Brought to their ears, while day declined:

— x. 99.

would either not accept
Life offered, or soon beg to lay it down,
Glad to be so dismissed in peace,

— xi. 507.

2 *xa* | *xx*:
Turning our tortures, into horrid arms
Against the torturer;

— ii. 64.

That golden sceptre, which thou didst reject,
Is now an iron rod, to bruise and break
Thy disobedience.

— v. 888.

adorned
With what all Earth or Heaven could bestow
To make her amiable!

— viii. 484

2 *xa* | *xxa*:
Hail, holy Light, offspring of Heav'n first-born,
Or of th' Eternal coeternal beam,
May I express thee unblamed?

— iii. 3.

Food not of Angels, yet accepted so,
As that more willingly thou couldst not seem
At Heav'n's high feasts to have fed :

— v. 467

           arms on armour clashing brayed
Horrible discord, and the madding wheels
Of brazen chariots raged ;

— vi. 211.

              yet oft they quit
The dank, and rising on stiff pennons tow'r
The mid aërial sky :

— vii. 442.

            the spirit of Man
Which God inspired, cannot together perish
With this corporeal clod !

— x. 786.

He looked, and saw a spacious plain, whereon
Were tents of various hue :

— xi. 557.

Then through the fiery pillar and the cloud
God, looking forth, will trouble all his host,
And craze their chariot-wheels :

— xii. 210.

xă | *xxă* | *xă* :
     Cherubic songs by night from neighb'ring hills
Aërial music send ;

— v. 548.

And now their mightiest quelled, the battle swerved,
With many an inroad gored :

— vi. 387.

          all the ground
With shivered armour strewn, and on a heap
Chariot and charioteer lay overturned,
And fiery foaming steeds :

— vi. 391.

      the crested cock, whose clarion sounds
The silent hours, and th' other whose gay train
Adorns him, coloured with the florid hue
Of rainbows and starry eyes.

— vii. 446.

x̌a | *x̌x̌a* :

> 'Twixt host and host but narrow space was left
> (A dreadful interval), and front to front
> Presented, stood in terrible array,
> Of hideous length.

—vi. 107.

> Forthwith from council to the work they flew ;
> None arguing stood ;

—vi. 508.

> Whence heavy persecution shall arise
> On all who in the worship persevere
> Of spirit and truth :

—xii. 533.

x̌a | *x̌x̌* :

> 　　　　　and th' ethereal mould
> Incapable of stain would soon expel
> Her mischief, and purge off the baser fire
> Victorious.

—ii. 142.

> 　　　　o'er which the mantling vine
> Lays forth her purple grape, and gently creeps
> Luxuriant :

—iv. 260.

> What meant that caution joined, If ye be found
> Obedient ?

—v. 514

> 　　　　and now went forth the morn
> Such as in highest Heav'n, arrayed in gold
> Empyreal ;

—vi. 14

> 　　　　　for what avails
> Valour or strength, though matchless, quelled with pain
> Which all subdues, and makes remiss the hands
> Of mightiest ?

—vi. 459.

> At his command th' uprooted hills retired
> Each to his place ; they heard his voice, and went
> Obsequious ;

—vi. 783.

4 *xo* | *x*:

> and joys
> Then sweet, now sad to mention, through dire change
> Befall'n us unforeseen, unthought of;
>
> — ii. 821.

> Son of my bosom, Son who art alone
> My word, my wisdom, and effectual might,
> All hast thou spoken as my thoughts are;
>
> — iii. 171.

> Forth flourished thick the clust'ring vine, forth crept
> The smelling gourd, upstood the corny reed
> Embattled in her field, and th' humble shrub,
> And bush with frizzled hair implicit.
>
> — vii. 323.

> One came, methought, of shape divine,
> And said, Thy mansion wants thee, Adam;
>
> — viii. 296.

2 *ax* | *xa*:

> My Author and Disposer, what thou bidst,
> Unargued. I obey; so God ordains;
> God is thy law, thou mine;
>
> — iv. 637.

The words 'God,' 'thy,' and 'mine' receive the stress.

> Nor yet in horrid shade or dismal den,
> Nor nocent yet, but on the grassy herb
> Fearless, unfeared, he slept.
>
> — ix. 187.

The prefix 'un-,' of 'unfeared,' receives the stress.

axx | *xa*:

> and as they went,
> Shaded with branching palm, each order bright,
> Sung triumph, and him sung victorious King,
> Son, Heir, and Lord, to him dominion given,
> Worthiest to reign.
>
> — vi. 883.

But Adam with such counsel nothing swayed,
To better hopes his more attentive mind
Labouring had raised ;

— x. 1013

a :
        now Conscience wakes Despair
That slumbered, wakes the bitter memory
Of what he was, what is, and what must be
Worse ;

— iv. 20.

           in his right hand
Grasping ten thousand thunders, which he sent
Before him, such as in their souls infixed
Plagues.

— vi. 838.

But if thou think, trial unsought may find
Us both securer than thus warned thou seem'st,
Go :

— ix. 372

Redouble then this miracle, and say,
How cam'st thou speakable of mute ; and how
To me so friendly grown above the rest
Of brutal kind, that daily are in sight !
Say !

— ix. 566.

xa | xxa | x :
For hot, cold, moist, and dry, four champions fierce
Strive here for mast'ry, and to battle bring
Their embryon atoms ;

— ii. 9**

     Nor was his ear less pealed
With noises loud and ruinous (to compare
Great things with small) than when Bellona storms
With all her batt'ring engines bent, to raze
Some capital city ;

· ii. 924

        unsav'ry food perhaps
To spiritual natures ;

v 402

With adverse blast upturns them from the south
Notus and Afer black, with thund'rous clouds
From Serraliona.

— x. 703.

ax | *xxa* | *xa* | *x*:

        Abashed the Devil stood,
And felt how awful goodness is, and saw
Virtue in her shape how lovely;

— iv. 848.

        I to thee disclose
What inward thence I feel, not therefore foil'd,
Who meet with various objects, from the sense
Variously representing;

— viii. 610.

3 *xa* | *xx*:

        That thou art happy, owe to God;
That thou continuest such, owe to thyself;
That is, to thy obedience:

— v. 522.

        but anon
Down cloven to the waist, with shattered arms
And uncouth pain fled bellowing.

— vi. 362.

xax | 2 *xa*:

        and with the setting sun
Dropt from the zenith like a falling star,
On Lemnos, th' Ægean isle:

— i. 746.

        my constant thoughts
Assured me, and still assure:

— v. 553.

This might be scanned as *xa* | *xxa* | *xa*. But, according to the construction, the other is better.

ax | *xa* | *xxa*:

        and forthwith light
Ethereal first of things, quintessence pure,
Sprung from the deep, and from her native east
To journey through the aery gloom began,
Sphered in a radiant cloud;

— vii. 247.

xa | *xxa* | 2 *xa* :

I heard thee in the garden, and of thy voice
Afraid, being naked, hid myself.

— x. 117.

xxa | *xa* :

Therefore what he gives
(Whose praise be ever sung) to Man in part
Spiritual, may of [1] purest Spirits be found
No ingrateful food :

— v. 407.

ax | *x* :

As far as Gods and heav'nly essences
Can perish ;

— i. 130

xa | *xxa* | *xa* | *x* :

The banded Pow'rs of Satan hasting on
With furious expedition ;

— vi. 86.

ax | *xxa* :

with grave
Aspéct he rose, and in his rising seemed
A pillar of state :

— ii. 302.

ax | *xa* | *ax* :

Not Spirits, yet to heav'nly Spirits bright
Little inferior :

— iv. 362.

xax :

nigh foundered on he fares,
Treading the soft consistence, half on foot,
Half flying ;

— ii. 942

axx | 3 *xa* :

but Eve
Undecked save with herself, more lovely fair
Than Wood-Nymph, or the fairest Goddess feigned
Of three that in mount Ida naked strove,
Stood to entertain her guest from Heav'n.

— v. 383.

---

[1] of : may have the force of ' by,' the antecedent being ' found ';
or, the antecedent may be ' food,' the meaning being, ' may be found
no ingrateful food of purest Spirits.' The former is the better.

axx | *ax* :

> he together calls,
> Or sev'ral one by one, the regent pow'rs,
> Under him regent :

— v. 698.

ax | 2 *xa* | *xxa* :

> These as a line their long dimension drew,
> Streaking the ground with sinuous trace ;

— vii. 481.

axx :

> Pleasing was his shape,
> And lovely : never since the serpent kind
> Lovelier :

— ix. 505.

ax | *xa* | *ax* | *xa* :

> In thy pow'r
> It lies, yet ere conception, to prevent
> The race unblest, to being yet unbegot.
> Childless thou art, childless remain :

— x. 989.

xxa | 2 *xa* :

> So both ascend
> In the visions of God.

— xi. 377.

The word 'visions' is trisyllabic. The remainder of the verse is ' It was a hill,' 2 *xa*.

2 *xa* | *ax* | *xa* :

> larger than whom the sun
> Engendered in the Pythian vale on slime,
> Huge Python, and his pow'r no less he seemed
> Above the rest still to retain.

— x. 532.

ax | 3 *xa* | *x* :

> This having learned, thou hast attained the sum
> Of wisdom : . . .
> . . . only add
> Deeds to thy knowledge answerable ;

— xii. 582

xa | *ax* | *x*:

        Both have sinned ; but thou
Against God only ;

               —x. 931.

The stress should be on the word 'God.'

xxa | *xa* | *x*:

Unskilful with what words to pray, let me
Interpret for him, me his Advocate
And propitiation.

            — xi. 34

xxa | *x*:

      (not so thick swarmed once the soil
Bedropt with blood of Gorgon, or the isle
Ophiusa) ;

            —x. 528.

xa | *ax*:

Was she thy God, that her thou didst obey
Before his voice ?

            — x. 146.

The word 'his' receives the stress.

To appreciate these varied sections of verses as contributing to the general melody and harmony of the verse, and to the special melody and harmony of the groups to which they severally belong, an entire book, at least, of the 'Paradise Lost,' should be read aloud at one time.

But no single reading is sufficient for the appreciation of the higher forms of verse, whatever those forms may be, any more than a single rendering, or a single hearing, of a production of the higher music is sufficient for its appreciation. A long familiarity is required for securing all the effects, consciously or unconsciously provided for, by the poet and the musical composer.

The second of the two grand features of Milton's blank verse I have mentioned, is the melodious and harmonious grouping of verses into periods or stanzas — larger or smaller waves of harmony, according to the propulsion of the thought and feeling which produces them.

The fusion of many of the larger groups is somewhat due to what may be called theme vowels and consonants ; certain vowels and consonants dominating throughout a group, and giving it a special vocal character, but not often so dominating as to be brought to the consciousness of the reader or hearer. There is much subtle initial and internal alliteration of consonants, which may pass entirely unnoticed, but which, nevertheless, contributes to the general melodious and harmonious effect of a group. This may be largely attributable to a fact already alluded to, that strongly esemplastic feeling, in the expression of itself, attracts certain vocal elements which best chime with, and serve to conduct, it.

In the following examples, I have given, generally, groups of average length, which the student can readily hold together, rather than long-sustained groups, of which the 'Paradise Lost' abounds in notable examples. As Matthew Browne [W. B. Rands], in his 'Chaucer's England,' remarks : 'The power of taking a long sweep before coming to a pause, and then beginning again with a spring from the pausing-point, is a well-known characteristic of the best poetry. It is a characteristic of which we had the last *magnificent* example in Milton.'

After citing Book i, 576–587, he adds: 'This is only a portion of the sentence, which in its complete form extends over seventeen lines of Milton's text

[571–587] ; but it will suffice to exhibit to the least
accustomed person, especially if he will read it out
loud, what is meant by length or strength of poetic
flight. It will be observed in reading it, that the
voice is kept in suspense, held as it were in the
air over the theme, and cannot come suddenly to
a cadence.'

The student should memorize all the examples
given, and afterwards frequently repeat them aloud,
until he completely feel the flow, and continuity, and
melodious cadence of each :

> 'Him the Almighty Power
> Hurled headlong flaming from th' ethereal sky,
> With hideous ruin and combustion, down
> To bottomless perdition, there to dwell
> In adamantine chains and penal fire,
> Who durst defy th' Omnipotent to arms.
>
> — i. 43-49.

> He scarce had finished, when such murmur filled
> Th' assembly, as when hollow rocks retain
> The sound of blust'ring winds, which all night long
> Had roused the sea, now with hoarse cadence lull
> Seafaring men o'erwatched, whose bark by chance
> Or pinnace anchors in a craggy bay
> After the tempest.
>
> — ii. 284-290.

> Then of their session ended they bid cry
> With trumpets' regal sound the great result :
> Tow'rds the four winds four speedy Cherubim
> Put to their mouths the sounding alchemy
> By herald's voice explained ; the hollow abyss
> Heard far and wide, and all the host of Hell
> With deaf'ning shout returned them loud acclaim.
>
> — ii. 514-520.

In discourse more sweet
(For eloquence the soul, song charms the sense)
Others apart sat on a hill retired,
In thoughts more elevate, and reasoned high
Of providence, foreknowledge, will, and fate,
Fixed fate, free-will, foreknowledge absolute,
And found no end, in wand'ring mazes lost.

— ii. 555-561.

Far off from these, a slow and silent stream,
Lethe, the river of oblivion, rolls
Her wat'ry labyrinth, whereof who drinks
Forthwith his former state and being forgets —
Forgets both joy and grief, pleasure and pain.

— ii. 582-586.

Through many a dark and dreary vale
They passed, and many a region dolorous,
O'er many a frozen, many a fiery Alp,
Rocks, caves, lakes, fens, bogs, dens, and shades of death —
A universe of death, which God by curse
Created evil, for evil only good,
Where all life dies, death lives, and nature breeds,
Perverse, all monstrous, all prodigious things,
Abominable, inutterable, and worse
Than fables yet have feigned, or fear conceived,
Gorgons and Hydras, and Chimeras dire.

— ii. 618-628.

I fled, and cried out *Death!*
Hell trembled at the hideous name, and sighed
From all her caves, and back resounded *Death!*

— ii. 787-789.

On a sudden open fly,
With impetuous recoil and jarring sound,
Th' infernal doors, and on their hinges grate
Harsh thunder, that the lowest bottom shook
Of Erebus.

— ii. 879-883.

No sooner had th' Almighty ceased but — all
The multitude of Angels, with a shout
Loud as from numbers without number, sweet
As from blest voices, uttering joy — Heaven rung
With jubilee, and loud Hosannahs filled
Th' eternal regions.

— iii. 344-349.

Sweet is the breath of Morn, her rising sweet,
With charm of earliest birds : pleasant the Sun,
When first on this delightful land he spreads
His orient beams, on herb, tree, fruit, and flower,
Glist'ring with dew; fragrant the fertile Earth
After soft showers; and sweet the coming on
Of grateful Evening mild ; then silent Night,
With this her solemn bird, and this fair Moon,
And these the gems of Heaven, her starry train :
But neither breath of Morn, when she ascends
With charm of earliest birds; nor rising Sun
On this delightful land ; nor herb, fruit, flower,
Glist'ring with dew; nor fragrance after showers;
Nor grateful Evening mild; nor silent Night,
With this her solemn bird; nor walk by Moon,
Or glitt'ring star-light, without thee is sweet.

— iv. 641-656

How often, from the steep
Of echoing hill or thicket, have we heard
Celestial voices to the midnight air,
Sole, or responsive each to other's note,
Singing their great Creator !

— iv. 680-684

At once on the eastern cliff of Paradise
He lights, and to his proper shape returns,
A seraph winged ; six wings he wore to shade
His lineaments divine : the pair that clad
Each shoulder broad came mantling o'er his breast
With regal ornament ; the middle pair
Girt like a starry zone his waist, and round

Skirted his loins and thighs with downy gold
And colours dipt in Heaven; the third his feet
Shadowed from either heel with feathered mail,
Sky-tinctured grain; like Maia's son he stood
And shook his plumes, that heavenly fragrance filled
The circuit wide.

—v. 275-287.

Meanwhile in other parts like deeds deserved
Memorial, where the might of Gabriel fought,
And with fierce ensigns pierced the deep array
Of Moloch, furious King, who him defied,
And at his chariot-wheels to drag him bound
Threatened, nor from the Holy One of Heaven
Refrained his tongue blasphèmous, but anon
Down cloven to the waist, with shattered arms
And uncouth pain fled bellowing.

—vi. 354-362.

They astonished, all resistance lost,
All courage; down their idle weapons dropt;
O'er shields, and helms, and helmed heads he rode
Of Thrones and mighty Seraphim prostràte,
That wished the mountains now might be again
Thrown on them, as a shelter from his ire.

—vi. 838-843.

On Heavenly ground they stood, and from the shore
They viewed the vast immeasurable Abyss
Outrageous as a sea, dark, wasteful, wild,
Up from the bottom turned by furious winds
And surging waves, as mountains, to assault
Heaven's highth, and with the centre mix the pole.

—vii. 210-215.

There was a place,
Now not, tho' sin, not time, first wrought the change,
Where Tigris at the foot of Paradise
Into a gulf shot under ground, till part
Rose up a fountain by the Tree of Life:
In with the river sunk, and with it rose

Satan, involved in rising mist, then sought
Where to lie hid; sea he had searched and land
From Eden over Pontus, and the pool
Mæotis, up beyond the river Ob;
Downward as far antarctic; and in length
West from Orontes to the ocean barred
At Darien, thence to the land where flows
Ganges and Indus: thus the orb he roamed
With narrow search, and with inspection deep
Considered every creature, which of all
Most opportune might serve his wiles, and found
The serpent subtlest beast of all the field.

— ix. 69-86.

So saying, through each thicket, dank or dry,
Like a black mist low creeping, he held on ·
His midnight search, where soonest he might find
The serpent: him fast sleeping soon he found,
In labyrinth of many a round self-rolled,
His head the midst, well stored with subtle wiles:
Nor yet in horrid shade or dismal den,
Nor nocent yet, but on the grassy herb
Fearless, unfeared, he slept.

— ix 179-187.

Thus saying, from her husband's hand her hand
Soft she withdrew, and, like a wood-nymph light,
Oread or Dryad, or of Delia's train,
Betook her to the groves; but Delia's self
In gait surpassed, and goddess-like deport,
Though not as she with bow and quiver armed,
But with such gardening tools as Art, yet rude,
Guiltless of fire, had formed, or Angels brought.

— ix. 385-392.

As one who, long in populous city pent,
Where houses thick and sewers annoy the air,
Forth issuing on a summer's morn, to breathe
Among the pleasant villages and farms
Adjoined, from each thing met conceives delight —

The smell of grain, or tedded grass, or kine,
Or dairy, each rural sight, each rural sound —
If chance with nymph-like step fair virgin pass,
What pleasing seemed, for her now pleases more,
She most, and in her look sums all delight.

— ix. 445-454.

So spake the Enemy of Mankind, enclosed
In serpent, inmate bad, and toward Eve
Addressed his way — not with indented wave,
Prone on the ground, as since, but on his rear,
Circular base of rising folds, that towered
Fold above fold, a surging maze ; his head
Crested aloft, and carbuncle his eyes ;
With burnished neck of verdant gold, erect
Amidst his circling spires, that on the grass
Floated redundant.

— ix. 494-503.

On the other side, Adam, soon as he heard
The fatal trespass done by Eve, amazed,
Astonied stood and blank, while horror chill
Ran through his veins, and all his joints relaxed :
From his slack hand the garland, wreathed for Eve,
Down dropt, and all the faded roses shed.

— ix. 888-893.

　　　　Immediately a place
Before his eyes appeared, sad, noisome, dark ;
A lazar-house it seemed, wherein were laid
Numbers of all diseased, all maladies
Of ghastly spasm, or racking torture, qualms
Of heart-sick agony, all feverous kinds,
Convulsions, epilepsies, fierce catarrhs,
Intestine stone and ulcer, colic pangs,
Demoniac phrenzy, moping melancholy,
And moon-struck madness, pining atrophy,
Marasmus, and wide-wasting pestilence,
Dropsies, and asthmas, and joint-racking rheums.

Dire was the tossing, deep the groans ; Despair
Tended the sick, busiest, from couch to couch ;

And over them triumphant Death his dart
Shook, but delayed to strike, though oft invoked
With vows, as their chief good and final hope.

—xi. 477–488; 489–493.

High in front advanced,
The brandished sword of God before them blazed
Fierce as a comet; which with torrid heat,
And vapour as the Libyan air adust,
Began to parch that temperate clime; whereat
In either hand the hastening Angel caught
Our lingering parents, and to the eastern gate
Led them direct, and down the cliff as fast
To the subjected plain — then disappeared.

— xii. 632–640.

Coleridge, in the third of his 'Satyrane's Letters,'
gives an account of his visit with Wordsworth to the
poet Klopstock. In the course of their conversation,
Klopstock talked of Milton and Glover, and thought
Glover's blank verse superior to Milton's. 'W——
and myself expressed our surprise; and my friend
gave his definition and notion of harmonious verse,
*that it consisted (the English iambic blank verse above
all) in the apt arrangement of pauses and cadences,
and the sweep of whole paragraphs,*

> *with many a winding bout
> Of linkèd sweetness long drawn out,*

*and not in the even flow, much less in the prominence
or antithetic vigor of single lines, which were indeed
injurious to the total effect, except where they were
introduced for some specific purpose.* Klopstock as-
sented, and said that he meant to confine Glover's
superiority to single lines.' He probably had not

appreciated any English blank verse beyond the individual line, if even so much as that.

Here we have what was probably the first true
characterization of Milton's blank verse given in
1798 or 1799. Mr. John Addington Symonds has
worked up this characterization in his article on the
blank verse of Milton in the 'Fortnightly Review,'
December 1, 1874, pp. 767–781, in which he states
that 'the secret of complex and melodious blank
verse lies in preserving the balance and proportion of
syllables while varying their accent and their relative
weight and volume, so that each line in a period shall
carry its proper burden of sound, but the burden shall
be differently distributed in the successive verses.'

De Quincey, in a somewhat humorous passage in
his essay entitled 'Milton *vs.* Southey and Landor,'
says : 'You might as well tax Mozart with harshness
in the divinest passages of "Don Giovanni" as Milton with any such offence against metrical science.
Be assured, it is yourself that do not read with un-
derstanding, not Milton that by possibility can be
found deaf to the demands of perfect harmony. You
are tempted, after walking round a line threescore
times, to exclaim at last, "Well, if the Fiend himself
should rise up before me at this very moment, in this
very study of mine, and say that no screw was loose
in that line, then would I reply, 'Sir, with submission, you are ——'" "What!" suppose the Fiend
suddenly to demand in thunder, "What am I?"
"Horribly wrong," you wish exceedingly to say;
but, recollecting that some people are choleric in
argument, you confine yourself to the polite answer,

"that, with deference to his better education, you conceive him to lie;"—that's a bad word to drop your voice upon in talking with a fiend, and you hasten to add, "under a slight, a *very* slight mistake." Ay, you might venture on that opinion with a fiend. But how if an angel should undertake the case? and angelic was the ear of Milton. Many are the *primâ facie* anomalous lines in Milton; many are the suspicious lines, which in many a book I have seen many a critic peering into with eyes made up for mischief, yet with a misgiving that all was not quite safe, very much like an old raven looking down a marrow bone. In fact, such is the metrical skill of the man, and such the perfection of his metrical sensibility, that, on any attempt to take liberties with a passage of his, you feel as when coming, in a forest, upon what seems a dead lion; perhaps he may *not* be dead, but only sleeping; nay, perhaps he may not be sleeping, but only shamming. And you have a jealousy, as to Milton, even in the most flagrant case of almost palpable error, that, after all, there may be a plot in it. You may be put down with shame by some man reading the line otherwise, reading it with a different emphasis, a different cæsura, or, perhaps, a different suspension of the voice, so as to bring out a new and self-justifying effect.'

Postscript on Some Blank Verse since Milton.

In regard to the blank verse produced since Milton, space will allow a reference only to some of the best. Sir Henry Taylor, in his letter to Sir John Herschel,

August 26, 1862 ('Correspondence,' edited by Professor Dowden), is hardly just in his estimate of it: . . . 'for more than a hundred years the art of writing anything but the heroic couplet seems to have been lost, . . . and when our verse ceased to clank this chain, it rose into lyrical movements of some force and freedom, but to me it seems never to have recovered the subtle and searching power and consonantal pith which it lost in that fatal eighteenth century, when our language itself was dethroned and levelled. The blank verse of Young and Cowper in the last century, or (with the exception of occasional passages) of Southey and Wordsworth in this, is, to my mind, no more like that of the better Elizabethans than a turnpike road is like a bridle path, or a plantation like a forest.'

Just what he meant to convey by the comparisons with which this extract concludes is not entirely evident; but that a too sweeping condemnation is involved of the blank verse produced since the Elizabethan era is evident enough.

The blank verse of Cowper's 'Task' is admirably adapted to the theme, which did not admit of a more elaborate style of verse. (The first ninety-five verses of 'The Winter Morning Walk' afford a good specimen of it.) Cowper saw further than any one before him had seen, into the secrets of the elaborate music of Milton's blank verse, and availed himself of those secrets to some extent — to as far an extent as the simplicity of his themes demanded. Whether he could have treated loftier themes in blank verse involving more of those secrets, is another question.

There are passages, however, in his translations of the 'Iliad' and the 'Odyssey' which indicate that he might well have done so, and make one regret that he wasted his time on Homeric translation.

The blank verse of Southey's 'Roderick, the Last of the Goths' has great merit as narrative verse, and is worthy of careful study. The variations on the theme-metre, and the resultant pause melody, show not only great metrical skill, but a moulding spirit which is quite a law to itself, and beyond mere skill.

Wordsworth's 'Yew Trees' is a bit of masterful blank verse which ranks with the very best in the language. His 'Lines composed a few miles above Tintern Abbey,' which announced the advent of a new gospel of poetry, have a charm peculiarly their own — a prevailing tone which is a radiation of the feeling embodied. The verse of his 'Nutting' and 'Michael' has a simplicity and directness, and an easy go, which are very charming. The blank verse of 'The Prelude' and 'The Excursion' is unequal in merit, there being a good deal of subject-matter in both compositions of a quality not demanding other than a prose expression; but they abound in specimens of blank verse of a high order.

The blank verse of Shelley's 'Alastor; or, the Spirit of Solitude' has an *animated* majesty which readers the least regardful of verse must feel and enjoy to some extent. The opening invocation to 'Earth, ocean, air, belovèd brotherhood!' extending to the forty-ninth verse; the verses enumerating the solemn places which the Poet's wandering step had visited (106–128); those descriptive of 'the ethereal cliffs of Caucasus'; of the cavern which 'ingulphed the rushing sea,' and its windings which the Poet's boat pursued; of the forest which he explored, 'one vast mass of mingling shade, whose brown magnificence a narrow vale embosoms' (351–468), are especially to be noted. But the verse throughout is very noble. Effective extra end-syllables crop out occasionally.

The blank verse of Matthew Arnold's 'Sohrab and Rustum' illustrates his own definition of the grand style, given in his essay 'On translating Homer': 'I think it will be found that the grand style arises in poetry *when a noble nature, poetically gifted, treats with simplicity or with severity a serious subject.'* A very comprehensive definition. If he had said, 'When one poetically gifted,' etc., omitting 'a noble nature,' the definition would have been imperfect. Simplicity and severity, in the treatment of a serious subject, demand a noble nature. They must be the expression of the poet's own moral constitution. In a poem which is largely the product of literary skill, and is not truly *honest* (the feeling being more or less affected), there is quite sure to be, in places, a greater or less strain of expression. High art (which is more than technique, and *must* involve the personality of the artist) is characterized by the absence of strain. 'Sohrab and Rustum' is absolutely without the slightest strain. Some readers may feel that there is too much of artistic restraint in it.

> Who reads this measure, flowing strong and deep,
> It seems to him old Homer's voice he hears.[1]

[1] Edith M. Thomas's sonnet 'After reading Arnold's Sohrab and Rustum.'

The cadence of the poem, which sets in at the 36th verse from the end, ' So, on the bloody sand, Sohrab lay dead,' has a sweet solemnity to which the movement of the verse contributes much.

The abundant extracts given in Section V. of this book, from Tennyson's ' Princess ' and ' Idylls of the King,' as examples of organic variety of measures, are sufficient to show his triumphant skill in the writing of blank verse. And the extract from his ' Enoch Arden,' on pages 6 and 7, is a notable example of it. His blank verse, too, has its own distinct character. It gives out no echoes of any of his great predecessors, so far as my own ears have heard. . It is an expression of his own poetic temperament.

Already in his ' Timbuctoo,' which took the Chancellor's medal at the Cambridge Commencement in 1829, when he was in his twentieth year, he showed a remarkable mastery over this most difficult form of verse.

But notwithstanding the high excellence of all the blank verse he has written, there is none, perhaps, superior to that of his ' Morte d'Arthur,' first published in 1842 (many years before the original ' Idylls of the King' were published), and afterwards incorporated in the concluding Idyll of the series, ' The Passing of Arthur.'   It is eminently noble.

All things considered, the greatest achievement of the century in blank verse, is Robert Browning's ' The Ring and the Book.'   I don't mean the greatest in bulk (although it *is* that, having 21,134 verses, double the number of the ' Paradise Lost ') ; I mean the greatest achievement in the effective use of blank verse in the treatment of a great subject — really the greatest subject, when viewed aright, which has been treated in English poetry — vastly greater in its bearings upon the highest education of man than that of the ' Paradise Lost.' Its blank verse, while having a most complex variety of character, is the most dramatic blank verse since the Elizabethan era. Having read the entire poem aloud to classes every year for several years, I feel prepared to speak of the transcendent merits of the verse. One reads it without a sense almost of there being anything artificial in the construction of the language ; and by artificial I mean *put consciously into a certain shape.* Of course, it *was* put consciously into shape ; but one gets the impression that the poet thought and felt spontaneously in blank verse. And it is always *verse* — though the reader has but a minimum of metre consciousness. And the *method* of the thought is always poetic. This is saying much, but not too much. All moods of the mind are in the poem, expressed in Protean verse.

Many other of Browning's poems (and they rank with his greatest productions) are in blank verse which, in each, has its own distinctly peculiar character. Among these should be especially noted, ' How it strikes a Contemporary ' (1855), ' An Epistle containing the strange medical Experiences of Karshish, the Arab Physician ' (1855), ' Fra Lippo Lippi ' (1855), ' Andrea del Sarto ' (1855), ' The Bishop orders his Tomb at St. Praxed's Church ' (1845), ' Bishop Blougram's Apology ' (1855), ' Cleon ' (1855), ' A Death in the Desert ' (1864), ' Caliban upon Setebos ' (1864),

'Mr. Sludge the Medium' (1864), 'Balaustion's Adventure' (1871).

All of these, with four exceptions, were published some years before Sir Henry Taylor pronounced his verdict upon the later blank verse. The verse of each is unique in character, and of eminent merit. But no one, however trained in verse, could appreciate it through a single reading. There are too many subtle effects provided for to be got at once.

He who adequately appreciates the verse of these poems, must regard Robert Browning as one of the greatest masters of language-shaping.

INDEX.

ADVERTISEMENTS.